Tio's
Protection

Tio's Protection

Lyric Bellamy

Archway Publishing books may be ordered through booksellers or by contacting:

Archway Publishing
1663 Liberty Drive
Bloomington, IN 47403
www.archwaypublishing.com
844-669-3957

ISBN: 978-1-6657-3131-7 (sc)
ISBN: 978-1-6657-3132-4 (e)

Library of Congress Control Number: 2022918257

Print information available on the last page.

Archway Publishing rev. date: 10/07/2022

Mature Content

PROLOGUE

"**Y**ou know that your tio loves you, right?" he asked

"Yes, Uncle Frankie. Forever and ever." She giggled.

"Yes, mi chica. Siempre y Siempre." He pulled the breastplate down to protect his body, then climbed on top of her and pinned her arms back. "Close your eyes."

She did as he instructed, shutting her eyes tight. She tried her best to relax her body, listening to his breathing and mapping out his next move in her mind as she had done a million times before. "Relax, mi chica."

Keeping her eyes shut, she completely relaxed her body.

"Good. Are you ready?" He asked.

She nodded her head yes.

"Go." He ordered.

She opened her eyes and started moving her arms and legs simultaneously, squirming to get from underneath him. He held her tight. She managed to squeeze her leg from underneath him and kneed him in the groin. He immediately let go of her arms and she used her elbow to hit him in the stomach. She went to gouge out his eyes, but the protective gear stopped her.

"Twenty seconds. Not bad." Uncle Frankie stood and hugged a beaming Alex. "But I know that you can knee harder than that. If you are ever attacked, you are to show no mercy, chica. None!"

"Si, tio," she said. "But you will always protect me, right, Uncle Frankie?"

He knelt and looked his eight-year-old niece in the eyes. She looked so much like her mother. After a moment of sadness, he answered her. "Yes, my heart. But if I am not around, I need you to promise me that you will remember everything that we have worked on. Every drill, every defensive move, everything!"

"But Uncle Frank-"

"Promise. Promesa!" he yelled.

"Promesa," she answered.

"I love you, my heart." He kissed the top of her head.

"I love you, too, Uncle Frankie." She held his hand as they walked down the hall of the mansion that sat in the middle of the sprawling 15-acre estate.

CHAPTER 1

Two years later

"Hey, Uncle Frankie." A bouncing ten-year-old Alexandria came into her uncle's office.

"My heart," Frankie replied while closing his laptop.

"Can we go to the movies and out for ice cream?" Alex made puppy dog eyes at her uncle.

He laughed. "Mi chica. We can watch whatever you like here and have ice cream delivered. Or I can have Chef make us some. It has been a while since you had some ice cream." He straightened the bow in her hair.

"I know, but I just want to go out. I get bored here by myself all the time," she pouted as she crawled into his lap.

"Last time you said you were bored, we ended up with Santos." As soon as Frankie spoke his name, Santos, a 200-pound golden brown English Mastiff barreled into the room, only stopping when Alex held up her hand.

She turned back to her uncle. "Santos is my best friend and I love him so much. It's just that sometimes I want to go out besides to school. I will be careful." Alex laid on the charm.

"I thought I was your best friend. You break my heart." Frankie placed his hands dramatically against his heart, causing Alex to laugh.

"You are, Uncle Frankie. I mean Santos is my second-best friend," she assured him. "I just want to go to the movies and for ice cream. Please? Por favor, tio?"

"Ok. Let me make some calls and finish up here. We will leave in an hour."

"Yes!" she squealed, causing Santos to become alert. Once he saw she was happy, he ran circles around her and then sat at her feet. She bent over to hug him.

"Take him outside to do his business before we go," Frankie said.

"Si, senor. Vamanos Santos." Alex and Santos left Frankie's office and took the elevator downstairs.

Picking up his phone, Frankie made a call. "Juan, we're going out to the movies and for ice cream. I need you to handle it."

"Si, jefe. No problem. Give me 20 minutes." Juan ended the call and got to work.

When they made it to the movies, Alex's face lit up with excitement, and that filled Frankie's heart. She looked at the various posters, smiling at each of them. Alex followed Frankie to the concession stand.

"Get whatever you want, my heart." Frankie kissed the top of the head.

"May I please get some nachos with cheese and extra peppers, some popcorn, a large drink, and a candy bar?" Alex gave the concessions attendant her order.

Frankie laughed. "And I will take a large drink as well, beautiful." The compliment from Frankie almost made the young lady's knees buckle. Frankie flashed her a smile that made her blush. Frankie was used to having that effect on women. He was 6'2", and 195 pounds of lean muscle and charisma. His naturally tanned skin, perfectly straight teeth, and chiseled facial features got him noticed by almost every woman he passed. Being 40 and having salt and pepper hair added to his sex appeal.

"Yes, yes sir. Can I get you anything else?" The young blonde stuttered. She looked to be around 21 years old, and her face was now red from blushing.

"Anything else, mi corazon?" Frankie asked Alex.

"No, senor. That's all." She smiled at her uncle.

"No, ma'am. That's all." Frankie paid for the concessions and then he and Alex headed towards their movie theater, followed by Juan, Dre, Marko, and Devon.

They entered their assigned theater and sat in the middle of their row. Frankie bought the remaining tickets to the 5:30 show, so there were only about thirty people in the movie theater, but Alex didn't mind. She was having the time of her life watching the animated dog movie on the screen. Frankie was enjoying the movie as well and was glad that Alex suggested they go.

"That was the best movie ever, Uncle Frankie. Thank you so much!" She hugged her uncle tight.

"Anything for you, my heart," he smiled.

"That was such a cool movie! Did you like it?" Alex asked.

"Yes, it was a pretty good movie." He opened the door of the SUV for her to climb in.

"I knew that you would like it!" Alex buckled her seatbelt, still excited about the movie.

After sharing ice cream at the new ice cream shop, Alex fell asleep on the way home. Juan drove them to the gate and nodded at the armed guard in the guard shack. The guard opened the gate and let them through. Frankie carried Alex up the front stairs of the mansion and into the house. He took the elevator to the second floor and carried her to her room. Santos was sitting outside her bedroom door, waiting for her return.

"Good boy," Frankie said as he opened the bedroom door to place Alex in her bed. Santos followed them into the room. Frankie removed her shoes and placed her under the covers, then gave her a kiss goodnight.

"I love you, my heart." He rubbed the top of Santos' head and exited her room. He found Juan waiting for him.

"Thank you for your efficiency. Alexandria means the world to me, and her happiness and safety is the most important thing to me." Frankie walked down the hallway towards the hidden door to the stairway.

"That's my job, boss. We have looked out for each other since we were sixteen-year-old outcasts trying to make a name for ourselves in the hood." He gave Frankie some dap. "But we do need to discuss some things. There has been talk of Cleo being up to his old tricks. Intel says that he's trying to make a move in some of your territories," Juan said as they walked up the hidden stairwell.

"Oh, our old friend, Cleo. Keep me posted on what he is up to." Frankie and Juan entered his office. Frankie went to the hidden panel in the wall and opened the safe. He pulled out four stacks of money and handed them to Juan. "For you and the others. Your loyalty means a lot. Ten thousand each for today. Gracias." Frankie shook Juan's hand.

"Gracias, jefe. We have a job to do, and we do it," Juan said as he placed the money inside his jacket.

"Si, we all have a job to do." Frankie walked Juan to the door. "I need a detailed report on Cleo in the morning."

"Si, jefe." Juan left the way he came.

Frankie sat at his desk and reclined in his chair. "That little weasel is going to make me get my hands dirty. What are you up to, now, Cleo?" Frankie was thinking out loud. He laughed to himself and made a few calls before bed.

CHAPTER 2

‌"C‌ome on, Santos!" Alex called out to Santos as he sniffed towards the wooded area at the very edge of the fenced property. "Santos, we are not supposed to go back this far," Alex whispered as she continued to follow Santos. The dog did something that he never did, which was ignore Alex and kept walking into the wooded area until he came to the huge brick wall covered in vines.

"Santos. Come on. Vamonos. Someone will see us." Alex tried to coax Santos back towards her. Santos looked at the top of the wall and started to growl. The hair stood up on the back of Alex's neck.

"Santos?" she whispered. The dog backed up towards Alex, still growling. He kept his body between Alex and the wall while backing her away from the wooded area.

"Hey, Alex. You aren't supposed to be back here," Tank said.

Alex, startled by Tank, started running towards him. "Tank, something is back there. Santos is growling at something."

Tank eased Alex behind him and aimed his assault rifle over the top of the wall, where Santos looked and still growled. Tank whistled and did a hand motion, signaling the other guards. Almost immediately four more guards were next to him with two canines.

"Alex, get back to the house. Now!" Tank ordered. Tank heard movement and barking on the other side of the wall, signaling that the other team and canines had something. Alex took off running and Santos followed behind her. She ran inside and she and Santos ran up three flights of stairs to Uncle Frankie's office. He opened the door just as she was about to burst through it. Juan ran out of the office door and to the elevator.

"Oh, mi Corazon. Are you ok? What happened?" He held onto a sobbing Alex.

"I don't know. Santos was growling at something, and he wouldn't come when I called him. He just kept growling. I'm sorry. I told him that we would be in trouble. I'm sorry, Uncle Frankie. I didn't mean to go back there, I just tried to get Santos."

"Shhh, my heart. You aren't in trouble. You are ok." He soothed her until she stopped crying. "I need you to do something for me."

Alex nodded her head "ok".

"I need you to take a deep breath and relax," Frankie said, and Alex obeyed. Sensing her new calmness, he spoke. "What did you feel?"

"Afraid. Muy asustado." Alex trembled, but she didn't cry.

"Then what should you have done?" Frankie asked calmly.

Alex took a deep breath and hung her head. Frankie raised her chin so that she could look him in the eyes. "Assess the situation. Look for something that I can use as a weapon. Run if it is the safest option. Fight if I have to, inflicting the most harm I can, but never get taken." Alex rehearsed what she had been taught since she was four years old.

"Si, Alexandria. Your actions today could have cost you your life," Frankie said sternly.

"But Santos…"

Frankie held up a finger to silence Alex. "If it is between you and Santos, it's always you! No exceptions."

"Si, tio," Alex responded.

"Now, mi Corazon, you and Santos go to your room. I will be there in a moment," Frankie ordered.

"Si, tio." Alex left his office, followed by Santos. Alex went into her room and climbed into her bed. Santos jumped in the bed with her and started licking her face. She snickered a little. "You almost got us in trouble, Santos." Santos placed his head in her lap, and Alex immediately rubbed his massive head and ears. "I love you, Santos," she said.

Juan and Dre entered Frankie's office, followed by Tank dragging a bloodied man by the collar of his shirt. Tank dropped the man in the middle of Frankie's office.

"We found him trying to flee the property," Juan said. Juan moved the collar on the man's shirt revealing a tattoo of a cross made by two guns on his neck. "This is one of Cleo's men. We are still trying to figure out how he got past the initial gate before he even made it to the wall."

Frankie's jaw twitched as he struggled to keep his anger at bay. He bent down in front of the bloodied man. "Tu nombre?"

The man laughed at Frankie. Frankie looked at Tank who bent down and punched the man in the jaw. Two of his teeth went flying across the room. The man moaned as blood oozed from his mouth.

Frankie spoke again. "Last time I will ask. What's your name?"

The man spit out blood before answering, "Jose."

"Good," Frankie replied. "Now what were you doing on my property? Huh?"

The man didn't reply, so Frankie held out his hand and Juan placed a gun in it. Frankie cocked it, stood, and pointed it at Jose.

"Wait, wait, wait." Jose held up his hands. "Look, I was just supposed to snatch the kid. That's all. I don't want to die, man. Cleo told me that I could make $50,000 by snatching her and delivering her to him. My mother and father are still in Mexico. They need the money. Man, please don't kill me," Jose pleaded.

Juan, Tank, and Dre took four steps back. They knew that the one thing that you never did was threaten or attempt to harm Alex. Frankie closed his eyes for a few moments before opening them again. "What did he want with her?" Frankie asked.

"I don't know. He just told me to snatch her and bring her to this address." Jose reached for his pocket, and the four men automatically drew on him. "You already got my piece and my phone. I don't have anything but this piece of paper on me. Just an address."

Frankie nodded for Jose to get the paper from his pocket. Juan took the paper, and Frankie spoke to Jose again. "What's your madre and padre's name?"

"Ramirez. Luciana Garcia and Ramone. From Guadalajara." Jose said.

"We have a problem, Jose. You threatened my heart, and well, there is nothing that I can do for you now." Frankie pointed the gun at Jose and emptied the magazine in him. He stepped over Jose's lifeless body and stood directly in Tank's face. "Who is responsible for letting this man get so close to my Alexandria? Was it you?" He held out his hand for another magazine to reload the gun. Juan handed him one. Frankie reloaded the gun and cocked it.

"Jefe, it wasn't me. We didn't know she was back there. I happened to see her as I made my rounds of the perimeter." Tank may have been as big as a Tank, but he was no fool. He knew that if he said the wrong thing, that he would be as dead as Jose.

"No disrespect, jefe, but he's right. Everyone was doing what they were supposed to do. He was the only one that spotted her," Juan said. Dre stood back, not saying a word.

Frankie walked back towards his desk and took his seat. "If anything like this happens again, I will empty this gun in your body."

"Si, jefe," Tank replied.

"Juan, look through his phone and call his mother. Send her the $50,000, and then dump this piece of shit at that address on the paper. It may be time for me to have a little chat with Cleo."

"Yes, boss." Tank picked up Jose's body and slung him over his shoulder. When they were gone, housekeeping came in to clean up the blood.

Juan waited until everyone was gone before he spoke to Frankie. "I also added ten more men to the grounds. Day and night there will be 14 guards patrolling at all times." He sighed. "Boss, you know that there is only one way he made it past the first gate."

"Si, amigo. Find out who let him in and kill him. Feed his body to the dogs."

"Si, jefe." Juan exited Frankie's office.

Frankie took the stairs to Alex's room. When he entered her room, she automatically sat up and apologized again. "Uncle Frankie, I'm sorry."

"It's ok, mi corazon." He took a seat on the bed next to her and Santos. "Remember the promise that we made each other? You promised that you would remember everything that we've went over. The drills and training."

"Yes." Alex said.

"And I promised you that I will always be here for you to protect you." Frankie countered.

"You sure did, Uncle Frankie." Alex smiled at him.

He rubbed her cheek. "So, we have to work together to keep our promises. You remember what you are supposed to do, and I will do what I am supposed to do. Right?"

"Right," Alex echoed.

"Good." Frankie patted her knee. "Now, get your gun and let's go practice."

"Yes, sir." Alex went to her bookshelf and pulled the faux book forward. A compartment popped out from the edge of the second shelf, and she retrieved her gun.

"Safety on?" Frankie asked.

Alex checked her gun. "Yes, sir." Alex tucked the small, hot pink compact .22 in the back of her pants like her uncle taught her. She and Santos followed Frankie to the elevator where the two of them took the elevator down to the basement. They went to the practice area where Frankie loaded a target for Alex in the shape of a man.

"Center mass. Go." Frankie ordered.

Alex removed the safety and did as she was told. Perfect shot, all ten times.

Frankie placed a loaded magazine on the table in front of her. "Head shots. Go."

Again, Alex made ten perfect shots.

"Good." Frankie turned on the sound bar and played background noise. Loud, distracting, background noise. He changed the target and pulled out the small, Glock 26 9 mm gun from the drawer, and sat two loaded magazines beside it.

"This target is different. You have two people here. Look carefully, mi Corazon. One is the enemy, one is your amiga. You have un minuto to decide. You are unfamiliar with this weapon. You have distractions all around you. Concentrate. Center mass then head shots. Go!"

Alex again did as she was told. As she loaded the magazine, she felt the weight of the gun, anticipating any kickback with each shot, and concentrated on her target, blocking out all distractions. Ten shots center mass, reloaded, then ten head shots. When she sat the gun down on the table, they both walked to the target on the other side of the basement. Perfect shots again. Frankie nodded.

"Buena chica. Tomorrow, we swap to heavier guns. We will also increase our defensive training and workouts," Frankie stated.

"Uncle Frankie, what's wrong? What happened outside today?" Alex asked as they walked back to the table of guns.

"Nothing for you to worry your pretty little head about, mi corazon. I'm handling it. I am here to protect you, and as long as I am alive, I'm all the protection that you will ever need." He kissed the top of her curly, jet-black hair.

"What about when you're no longer alive? Who will protect me then?" Alex's eyes watered at the thought of losing the only family she had.

"Don't cry, my heart." Frankie wiped away her tears. "I have that taken care of as well. You know what to do if you're ever in trouble?"

Alex nodded and wiped away the remaining tears that fell from her eyes, then straightened her shoulders like her uncle taught her.

"Hey, when did you get so tall? You're growing like a weed," he kidded with her.

"I know. I'm growing. I am almost 5 feet tall." She stuffed her gun in her pants as they walked back to the elevator. "Was my mother tall?"

Frankie hesitated for a moment before answering her. "No, mi corazon, she wasn't very tall. Maybe 5 foot 4 inches. You will be much taller than she was." They stepped onto the elevator.

"I wish I could have met her. And mi padre," Alex said.

"She was a great woman who loved you very much." Frankie didn't bother to comment on the father part.

"Do I look like her?" Alex asked as they exited the elevator and met a waiting Santos.

"Yes, my dear. Very much so. Our father was Mexicano. My mother was also Mexicana, but she was murdered when I was three years old. Mi padre and I went to California to visit family, and that is where he met your grandmother. She was black. Mi padre fell in love and asked her to marry him. She was the best madre I could have asked for. It was hard for her living in Mexico with us, being the only black person around, but she stayed because she loved us and treated me like I was her own." Frankie and Alex walked into her room and sat on her bed. Frankie had told her this story a thousand times, but Alex loved hearing about her family history. Frankie continued. "I was eight when your mother was born. She was the most beautiful baby I had ever seen. Her skin was the color of caramel, and she had that curly jet-black hair just like you." Frankie smiled. "Mi madre and padre let me name her."

"And you named her Adriana." Alex smiled.

"Yes, I did. It was my job to protect her like I do you. When I was fifteen years old, my father was murdered. Carolyn took me and

Adriana and fled back to California. She said that she would never leave me behind because she loved me and I was her son, too."

"What happened to the people that killed mi abuelo?" Alex asked as she put her gun back in its secret place.

"When I was old enough, I took care of them. I went to school for my education, and then I picked up where my father left off. My mother never knew, she would have been disappointed. She always said that the lifestyle that took her husband's life wouldn't take her son's." Frankie chuckled at the memories of the woman he considered his mother, Carolyn. "That is why I work so hard, so you will never have to do what I do, and so that I will not have to do this forever. You are going to go to school and become a doctor like you have dreamed of being."

"I know, Uncle Frankie." Alex sat next to her uncle and placed her head on his shoulder. "What about my mother dying?"

"A car accident. It was raining and she went to get some diapers for you. I told her I would go, but she said that she would be right back. A driver lost control of their car, hit her, knocking her off the cliff. And from that day to this one, I promised my dying mother and myself that I would always keep you safe."

"I love you, Uncle Frankie." Alex hugged her uncle.

"I love you, too, my heart." Frankie held her tight.

CHAPTER 3

‖‖

"Long time no hear, Frankie."

"Did you get your trash delivery, Cleo?" Frankie spat into the phone.

Cleo laughed. "That was my bad. I shouldn't have sent a boy to do a man's job."

"Oh, and what job is that?" Frankie asked.

"Frankie, cut the bullshit. Why are you calling me?" Cleo asked.

"Just to let you know that if you want war, I will give you one. Este es un-"

"I don't speak Spanish mother fucker. What are you trying to say?" Cleo yelled in the phone.

Frankie clenched his fists and then unclenched them. "This is a war that you can't win. Don't threaten my family or my livelihood again, and it's all good. If you come at me or my family again, I will kill you myself," Frankie spoke calmly.

Cleo laughed again. "Man, you always did think that you were better than everyone else. I think you called us common thugs." Cleo laughed again. "You got that flunky De'Juan doing all your dirty work. Tell him I said he ain't Mexican. His name is De'Juan, not Juan.

What we have will never be over. I will never stop coming for you. Do you hear me? You are just a wetback that a black lady felt sorry for and raised."

Frankie felt his blood boil.

"How is she? Oh, yeah. Dead. And your sister. Trust me ese, you are next. Then who will be there for that pretty little niece of yours? In a few years she will make a good little-"

"I am going to fucking kill you! Do you hear me? I am going to kill you!" Frankie yelled into the phone.

Cleo just laughed. "Like you killed my brother? And my son? Huh? Payback is a mother fucker. Sleep with both eyes opened because reparation day is coming." Cleo ended the call and looked at his right-hand man, Trig. "Jose did exactly what I thought he would do, get caught. Tell everybody to stay ready. Soon, we move in and take down Frankie Pena. All you mother fuckers better remember that I get to kill that bitch Frankie myself."

"Yes, sir." Trig said as he went to inform the others of the next move.

Frankie pounded his fists on his desk. "Fuck, fuck, fuck." He took a deep breath to calm himself and get his thoughts in order. He dialed Juan's number.

"Juan, where are you?" Frankie asked.

"Outside with Alex and Santos. What's up?" Juan asked.

"Do not alarm Alex. I need you inside, but make sure that Alex is guarded before you come up." Frankie ended the call and stood at the window to look for Alex. He saw her playing with Santos in the front yard. He smiled and wished that he could provide her with a childhood that was more carefree than anything else in the world. Instead, he had to raise a little girl that could be a killer if she needed to be.

"Boss, you needed me?" Juan said as he entered the office.

Frankie turned to Juan and spoke. "I spoke to Cleo. He is hell bent on killing me and wanting war. Tell everyone to move quietly and pack extra heat. No one moves alone, and keep their eyes opened. I need everyone to be on alert here at the house at all times. Did you ever find out who the traitor is?"

"Not yet, jefe. I'm still working on it. In the meantime, I need you to change your passcodes, and only you, Alex, and I will know them," Juan said.

Frankie side-eyed Juan for a moment. "Are you the traitor? Is it you that betrayed me?" Frankie stood.

"Look who you are talking to. It's me, Frankie. I'm telling you this as a friend. We don't know who we can trust at this very moment, and I don't want to take a chance on your safety or Alex's. You are like a brother to me, man. "You both are the only family that I have," Juan stated.

"You're right. I'm sorry. I know that you would never betray me, but I need to find out who did. And soon." Frankie walked to the door and Juan followed.

"Yes, boss." Juan said as he followed Frankie down the stairs.

Frankie opened the front door and called Alex inside.

"Yes, sir. Come on Santos." Alex and Santos both ran into the house, Santos going straight for his water bowl.

When Alex entered the house, Frankie grabbed her arm and started to pull her backwards. She grabbed his wrist, twisting it while she spun out of his grasp and jabbed him in the side.

"Ahh!" Frankie yelped. "Good girl. Always alert. You are getting stronger." Frankie rubbed his side and rolled his wrist around in a circle.

"I'm sorry, Uncle Frankie. You startled me." Alex looked like she was about to cry.

"No, no, my heart. You did what you were supposed to do. Great job." He held up his hand for a high five.

Alex smiled and high fived him. "Did I hurt you?" She asked.

"Not like you could have," he replied. "Come on, we need to talk."

Alex followed Frankie into the kitchen where he handed her a bottle of water and got one for himself. They sat at the kitchen island and Frankie sighed. "I have always tried to take care of you and protect you. I want to let you know that there will be some changes coming our way. We are changing all the codes and will have more security. No matter what, I still want you to be a child, and still smile and play like you were doing today." He reached out and held her hand.

"Can you tell me what's going on? Maybe I can help," Alex asked enthusiastically.

"I never want you to worry, you deserve better than that. There is just a man trying to cause us trouble, but I have it under control. We didn't do your boxing lessons today. You ready?" he asked.

"Yes! I love boxing!" Alex hopped down from the island and headed down the stairs to the basement. Frankie was right behind her.

The next few weeks were mostly filled with the same things. Frankie and Alex woke up at five in the morning for their workouts and runs. They had breakfast and then they got dressed to take Alex to school.

"Adios, tio. Love you." Alex kissed Frankie on the cheek.

"Adios, mi corazon." Have a great day. I love you." Frankie watched as Alex filed in line with the other students entering the building. When he got back into the SUV, he asked Juan if they have heard anything from Cleo.

"No, boss. We haven't heard anything. None of the distro sites have been hit. Nothing. No alarm or problem at the house either. No one has heard from or seen him." Juan merged into traffic.

Frankie looked out of the window, wondering what Cleo was up to. "We still cannot let down our guard."

"Got it." Juan said.

"Still no word on the inside man?" Frankie asked.

"Nope, none." Juan continued driving.

Frankie made a mental note to investigate who betrayed him because Juan didn't seem too eager to find out.

At recess, Alex played kickball with her friends. "Come on, Katie. Kick it hard!" Alex shouted from second base.

Katie smiled at Alex and kicked at the ball as hard as she could and missed. Everyone laughed at Katie except Alex.

"Come on, Katie. You can do it." Alex cheered her on again. She saw a jogger run past the school fence. She thought it odd but didn't give it too much thought. Katie kicked the ball and Alex ran to third base and then home. Her teammates cheered her on. After high fiving everyone, she made her way back to the end of the line. Alex noticed the jogger run by again, and then stop to stretch. The hairs on her neck stood up. Instead of cowering, and letting him know that she noticed him, she stood there cheering as she took note of his appearance.

5'8"-5'10" tall, white male, brown hair, brown eyes, gun tattoo that forms a cross on his neck. Scar on his left arm. Pointy nose and a mustache. Black shorts, white shirt, earbuds, black shoes.

She continued to take in his features as she pretended to yell for her teammates. The jogger bent down to tie his shoe.

"Yo, I think I see her." The jogger said through his earpiece as he pulled his phone out of his pocket and looked at the picture that was sent to him.

"What does she have on?" The person on the other end of the phone asked.

"Same as all the other girls, dumbass. A school uniform. But she has two ponytails with white ribbons in her hair. There are only about six black girls in the school, two in her grade. It's her." The jogger said.

"Ok. The school bell rings in thirty minutes. Grab her before they come to pick her up." The person on the other end said.

"Got it." The jogger stood and continued with his run.

Alex noticed the man's lips moving, like he was talking to someone. The coach blew the whistle, signaling it was time to go back to class and pack up to go home. Alex took her place in line and entered the building and then went to class. When she got to class, she slipped her phone in her pocket and asked her teacher if she could go to the bathroom. She went into the stall and pulled out her phone.

New project at school that I am working on, and Mrs. Stevenson needs me to help load up her car.

Alex waited impatiently for her uncle to reply.

Cool. See you in a bit.

Alex walked out of the bathroom stall and looked in the mirror. She took a deep breath to calm herself. It may not be anything, but her uncle always told her to trust what she feels, and she felt alarmed. She took her two ponytails down and put her hair in one ponytail and removed the ribbons from her hair. She walked back to class and grabbed her things, waiting on the bell. The bell rang and Alex took her time making her way out front to the pickup line. She noticed the jogger standing around where the parents were as they waited for their kids. He changed into khaki pants and a polo shirt.

"Alex, are you ok?" Mrs. Stevenson asked.

"Yes, ma'am. I was just making sure that I remembered my homework for tonight. Page 76, right?" she asked Mrs. Stevenson, buying herself some time.

"You got it, sweetie. Go ahead and get in the pickup line." Mrs. Stevenson looked outside when she heard a scream.

The jogger had grabbed Kenya, Alex's classmate before he realized it wasn't Alex. As she screamed, he ran off, being chased by school security. Mrs. Stevenson ran outside to check on Kenya. Alex turned and exited the school into the faculty parking lot where Juan and Frankie waited for her. She ran to the SUV and hopped in.

"What happened?" Frankie asked.

"He tried to grab Kenya. He thought it was me. I know he did." Alex was taking deep breaths in and out.

"Are you sure?" Frankie asked as Juan pulled out of the parking lot.

"I'm sure. She wore two ponytails today, too. We are almost the same height and the same color. I took my ponytails down. He was looking for me. Why Uncle Frankie? Who was it?" Alex refused to cry.

"Someone who wants to hurt me by taking away the one thing that I love," he said.

"Me?" Alex questioned.

"Yes, mi corazon. You." Frankie answered coolly and calmly, but inside he was fuming.

"But why? Is he trying to kill me?" she asked in a quivering voice.

"I won't let him." Frankie tapped his fingers on his knee.

Alex took a deep breath and hoped she wasn't out of line by saying this. "Why don't you kill him first?"

Frankie snapped his head to the side to look at her, but he didn't answer her. Alex looked out of the window for the rest of the ride home. No one spoke, everyone deep in thought. When they made it home, Frankie ordered Alex to go straight to her room and change out of her uniform. Santos followed her up the stairs.

"That mother fucker has lost his mind." Juan said. "Sending someone to her school. How did he know where she attended school? He must be watching her. Watching us."

"Or his inside man told him. Tell me, hombre, how is it that it has been a month since Jose breached these walls, and you still don't have any idea of who it was? Why? Por que?" Frankie yelled at Juan.

"Hey man, I'm trying. I have a plan. I'm just waiting for him to show his cards. You keep saying that shit like you think I did it." Juan raised his voice back at Frankie.

"Are you? I mean we have changed up everything; different routes, different codes, and they still found a way to get close to her." Frankie said in an accusatory tone.

Alex made her way down the stairs and towards the kitchen but stopped when she heard them talking. She made Santos stop and sit.

"Frankie, man, that wasn't me. You want to put the blame on everyone except where it belongs. You! You killed his brother and his son, and tried to kill him, too. You knew that he survived, and it was just a matter of time before he wanted blood for blood," Juan said.

Alex stayed out of sight as she listened.

"No, mi amigo. Los matamos." Frankie countered.

"Yeah, **we** did kill them. We, because where you go, I go. A threat to you is a threat to me. I will never forget how you took on every kid on the block when they jumped me, or how when my momma died from an overdose and I had nowhere else to go, your mother took me in. I think about that shit every day! Hermanos. Or did you forget?" Juan was in Frankie's face.

"Hermanos." Frankie said, and Juan relaxed and stepped back. "Brothers, yes. I'm sorry. I did not forget. I'm just frustrated. But brother or no brother, if you step in my face like that again, I will knock you on your ass."

Juan laughed. "I'm sorry, boss, and I know that you will." They hugged it out. "So, what's the plan?"

"Cut the head off the snake." Frankie said.

"I'm ready, Uncle Frankie. What are we about to do?" Alex walked into the kitchen where Frankie and Juan were.

"Alex, I want you to take down Juan." Frankie pointed to Juan.

"What the hell? How?" Juan asked.

Alex smirked at Juan and turned to Frankie. "Yes, sir."

The three of them took the stairs to the basement.

"I'm afraid that I have become too easy of an opponent for her. She needs someone new to take on." Frankie smiled at Alex, and she smiled back.

"You're serious? Frankie, I don't want to hurt her. I'm at least a foot and a half taller, eighty pounds heavier, and a man." Juan looked at Frankie like he lost his mind.

"Are you scared?" Frankie asked.

"No, boss. Ok. Let's go. I won't hurt her." Juan said.

He stepped to Alex and grabbed her around the neck. Alex was caught off guard and admittedly thought that he was faster than she anticipated. He applied pressure to her neck, and she elbowed him in the side as she pushed her chin into his arm, maneuvering a few inches to the side. She grabbed his arm, and she went to kick him in the groin. He released his grip to block her foot, and she used the palm of her hand to strike him in the nose. He stumbled back and wiped his bloody nose. The entire confrontation lasted all of ten seconds.

"I think you broke my nose," he said.

"I hope she did," Frankie said and laughed. He turned to Alex. "Not every opponent will feel your hits. Did you notice how he still had a grip on your neck after you elbowed him?"

Alex nodded her head yes and rubbed her neck.

"Let me see." Frankie turned her head to the side to look at the bruising on her neck. "Yeah, it is going to leave a mark."

"It's ok. It's just a lesson learned," Alex replied.

"I'm going to get my nose checked out. I will holler at you later, jefe." Juan took the stairs to the upper level.

"No school for you tomorrow. I have something that I need to do," Frankie said.

CHAPTER 4

Alex, Frankie, and Juan all entered the SUV to drive to school like they always did. They pulled out of the gate and took the route that they always took, except for one turn. They pulled off on a side street where there was another waiting SUV driven by Dre. The second SUV pulled out and continued the route. Dre drove the school route, and as they suspected, a black car appeared behind him. When Dre changed lanes, the car changed lanes.

"Yep, that's them," he said into his earpiece.

"Keep driving," Frankie said into the phone as Alex got out of the SUV and into a waiting car with Tank. "I will be back, mi corazon." Frankie kissed Alex on her forehead.

"Be careful, tio. I love you." She hugged him tight.

"I love you." He shut the car door and got back into the SUV with Juan.

"Dre, what's going on now?" Frankie asked.

"They are speeding up beside me. I think they are gonna try to shoot. Dumbasses." Dre laughed.

Frankie laughed, too. "Did they think that I would take Alex around in a car that wasn't bulletproof?"

"Obviously. Ok. They are beside me now, looking in. Looking for her, I'm sure. I'm about to stop at the light on Main Street. What do you want me to do?" Dre asked as he cocked the gun in his lap.

"We are three cars behind you. Keep straight where there is less traffic." Frankie said.

"Si, jefe." Dre pulled off when the light turned green. Like Frankie said, the farther he went out, the less traffic there was, until there was none. The car sped up beside Dre and tried to shoot at him.

"Yeah, they tried it." Dre said.

"I see them." Frankie said. "Pull over."

Dre pulled over and the car slowed down to pull over behind him. They didn't see Juan speeding towards them. He hit them so hard that the car spun around a couple of times before coming to a stop on the side of the road near the SUV that Dre was in. Juan, Frankie, and Dre got out and walked to the car, guns drawn. The passenger looked like he hit his head on the window and was unconscious, and the driver was reaching under the seat for his gun.

"Sit up," Juan said.

The man complied, putting his hands up in the air.

"What were you looking for?" Juan asked.

The driver didn't say anything. Juan cocked his gun and put it to his head. "Let me ask you again. What were you looking for?"

"You know what I was looking for. The girl," the driver said.

"Why?" Frankie asked.

"You know why," the driver said. "An eye for an eye. Street justice."

"Yeah, street justice." Frankie said as he emptied the gun into the driver. Juan pushed him over onto the unconscious passenger and got in the car. He drove to the lake where he and Dre pushed the car in and watched it sink.

"Maybe we should have killed the passenger, too," Dre said.

"He isn't a concern of mine. If he wakes up and survives, good for him. If not, well, he has the same fate as his friend," Frankie said as they walked back to the SUV with Juan.

"Now to sniff out the rat," Juan said as they pulled off and drove back to a waiting Alex and Tank.

"Tio!" Alex jumped out of the car and ran to Frankie. She felt all over his body like she was looking for bullet holes.

"I'm fine, and in one piece, mi corazon," Frankie said.

"Just making sure. Can we go home now?" Alex asked as she held his hand.

"Si." He opened the door of the SUV for her to climb in and they drove back to the house.

They pulled to the front door where Alex got out and walked into the house. Juan took notice to see which, if any of the men seemed to be surprised or take special notice of Alex being at home instead of school. *One, two, three.* Juan counted the men in his head as she entered the house.

"Uncle Frankie, I was thinking that I should just be tutored here instead of going back to school. That way I can be here with you," Alex said as she ate her bowl of fruit.

"You need to be around other children. You don't want to be with me day in and day out," Frankie replied.

"Yes, I do." Alex countered.

"Well, we will talk about it later. Change your clothes and then we can go outside and play with Santos." Frankie ordered.

"Si, senor," Alex said as she bound up the stairs.

"We will know in a minute who it was. I will be outside if you need me," Juan told Frankie as he headed back outside.

"Ok." Frankie took the stairs to his office to wait on Alex.

Walking around the corner of the house, he answered his phone. "Hello."

"Where in the fuck is Rico and Maine?" Cleo shouted from the other end of the phone.

"How in the fuck am I supposed to know? She is back at the house. Obviously, they don't have her," he said.

"Fuck this shit." Cleo hung up the phone.

"Fuck," he said.

"Everything, alright, man?" Juan asked.

"Yeah, man. My old lady riding my nuts about spending time with her. You know how it is," he said.

"Yeah, no doubt," Juan said before turning to walk away and answer his phone. He sprinted in the house to get to Frankie.

Alex put on her tennis shoes and a black shirt with her jeans. She pulled her hair back into a ponytail and hummed as she hung her uniform back in the closet. She looked out of her window to see commotion towards the front yard. All the guards were running towards the gate. Santos sat up and looked at Alex.

Juan ran into Frankie's office. "Man, all the distro sites have been hit simultaneously. No warning, they just came in blasting."

"Que?" Frankie asked.

"And the rat is Marko. It's fucking Marko." Juan and Frankie ran to the window when they heard gunshots. Frankie and Juan saw their men exchanging gunfire with another group of men. Juan went to the bar at the corner of the room and pushed the button to reveal an arsenal of weapons. He got an automatic rifle and a Glock 9. "Get Alex and stay here." As Juan opened the door, Alex and Santos ran in.

"Uncle Frankie!" Alex said as she ran into his arms.

Juan shut and locked the door behind him.

Juan didn't make it down the hallway before they heard gunshots. Frankie went to the bar, grabbed a gun, and handed it to Alex, and then got two for himself. He hit the corner of the desk to open the false side and put Alex in it. "Mi corazon, I love you. You know what to do. Don't look or turn back." Frankie's voice cracked as he hit the corner again to close Alex inside.

Santos started growling at the door and a few seconds later there was a knock.

"Knock, knock mother fucker." Cleo called.

Frankie didn't answer. Cleo motioned for his men to kick in the door and after three attempts they kicked it in. The first man entered and was shot dead by Frankie. The second man came in and Santos went for his throat. He shot Santos, but Santos didn't let go until the man was lifeless, his blood covering Santos's face. The next man shot at Frankie and missed. Frankie then caught him between the eyes before being shot by Cleo.

"Ahhh!" Frankie yelped and dropped his gun.

Alex covered her mouth to keep the sound from escaping as the tears ran down her face.

"Finally, Frankie Pena and I are face to face, again." Cleo said.

Frankie reached for his gun, but Cleo kicked it away. He held his side as blood gushed from his open wound.

Cleo bent down in front of Frankie. "You killed my son and my brother, and you tried to kill me. I took six bullets that night. I wonder everyday why I survived. Now I know it was so I could kill you." Cleo hit Frankie in the head with the butt of his gun. "Do you know what it's like to see your child murdered? You see that shit every time you close your eyes to go to sleep."

"Your brother and son were pigs. They tried to rape my sister. I would kill them again if I could," Frankie said.

"Shut your ass up." Cleo hit him again. "They were drunk and high. Fucked up. They would have never tried that shit otherwise."

"If I didn't happen to come by that night, there is no telling what they would have done to her! Your brother and your son," Frankie tried to sit up but doubled over in pain again.

Santos tried to get up from the corner but fell back down and whimpered. Alex remained still and quiet under the desk.

"I loved your sister, you know. At one point, I even considered you my brother-in-law, until you did what you did." Cleo spat the words at Frankie.

"Love? You used to beat her. I wish I would have known before that night that you put your hands on her, and I would have attempted to kill you sooner," Frankie said defiantly. He noticed that the gunfire was starting to die down.

"Ok. Whatever. This has gone on way too long. Tell me where my daughter is," Cleo demanded.

"Vete a la mierda!" Frankie said.

"No, fuck you, Frankie." Cleo shot Frankie in the chest and watched his lifeless body slump against the floor.

"Shit." Cleo said as Juan turned to corner and fired at him. "I thought you were dead, De'Juan," Cleo said.

"Hell naw! I can't die until you are dead." Juan shot two more times at Cleo until his gun was empty. "Fuck," he whispered. He didn't have another magazine or gun.

"Sounds like you are out, De'Juan. Time for you to die just like your boss, Frankie." Cleo turned the corner to shoot Juan, but he was gone.

Alex waited until it was quiet around her, and she heard the cars pull off. She pushed the button on the inside of the desk and cocked the gun that Frankie had given to her. She peered from around the desk and saw her uncle's lifeless body. She crawled to him and put his head in her lap.

"Nooo!! Nooo!! Wake up, Uncle Frankie. Wake up! No! Don't leave me!" She wept over his lifeless body. She kissed his cheek and tucked the gun in the back of her pants. She wiped her tears as she crawled over to Santos.

He gave her a small whimper and she smiled. "Santos. You're alive." He tried to wag his tail. "Santos, we have to hurry before they come back. We have to go." She tried to move him but couldn't. She cried. "No, Santos. No! I can't leave you, too. I need you to try to crawl for me or try to walk. Please, Santos! Please!" Santos tried to stand. He cried out and whimpered as he limped to the desk. She helped pull him underneath the desk and pushed the button to close the door and lower them to the basement. Santos whimpered as they slowly went down the shaft. The system was not built to carry almost three hundred pounds with them both. The pulley creaked and rocked until it landed with a thud at the basement floor. Santos let out a loud yelp before tumbling out of the shaft when Alex opened the door.

Alex went to the hidden door on the wall and pushed to open the door to the tunnel. She looked frantically for something to help her carry Santos down the tunnel. She found a flatbed cart and put a blanket on it before helping Santos get on it. His breathing was heavy, and Alex knew that he was running out of time. After he was loaded on the cart, Alex started to push him towards the hidden door. She heard the basement door open and then footsteps. Alex used all her strength to get Santos through the door and then closed it. She pushed Santos to the halfway point and got the bag that Frankie put in the wall compartment for her. She pulled out the cellphone, selected the only saved contact, and pressed the call button.

Winston's Veterinarian Services, please leave a message.

"Hey, Aunt Vy. A rabid fox got into the chicken coop and killed them. The dogs tried to fight him off, but they ended up getting bit, too. We really need you to come by and look at them, you know, let us know if there is any light at the end of the tunnel. We will be waiting." Alex hung up the phone and cried. When she closed her eyes, all she could see was her uncle's lifeless body and hearing Cleo call her his daughter. She took a deep breath to calm her nerves. She went through the packed bag and found a bottle of water. She took a sip and then poured a little in Santos's mouth. He tried to use his tongue to lap it up but couldn't. Alex made sure that everything was in the bag that she needed, and it was. Taking a deep breath, she continued to push Santos through the tunnel. After making it to the end, she peered through the peephole of the door and didn't see anything. She sat and waited. The sun went down, and Alex checked on Santos again. He was breathing, but barely. She poured a little more water in his mouth and rubbed his belly as she hummed a song to him.

When she woke up and looked out of the peephole. It was daylight and still, no one came. She slid down against the wall and spoke to Santos. "I'm sorry, boy. I tried to get you help. I tried to save you, but I think that we both may die right here unless I leave to get us some help." Santos didn't even make a sound. Alex tried to think. She knew that once the door shut, she could not open it again from the other side, and the tunnel took her fifty yards away from the gate that ran the perimeter of the property. If she opened the door and left it propped open, she risked being caught or found if Cleo and his men were still out there. A noise from outside brought Alex out of her thoughts. She looked through the peephole and saw a black SUV pull up to the designated spot and a woman got out. She stood at the front of the SUV and gave the hand signal. Alex took in her appearance. She was a beautiful brown woman with her hair pulled back into a ponytail. She was wearing a pair of black boots, blue jeans, and a black shirt. Alex saw the woman look to her left and hold her hands up as a guy approached her with a gun. Alex placed her ear to the door so that she can try to hear what was going on.

"Please sir, I'm just lost. I pulled over to try and call for directions." The lady held her hands up in front of her.

"What's a pretty little thing like you doing out here? It's not safe, you know." One of Cleo's men walked up to her and ran his hand across her chest, down her back, and then grabbed her ass. He leaned in to sniff her neck. "And you smell good, too." The man licked her neck.

The lady eased her hand into her pocket, pulled out a knife and jammed it into his throat. She moved the blade from right to left, twisting the man so that the blood sprayed outward, not getting any blood on her. The man fell in a heap at her feet, and the woman kicked him over. Alex put her bag over her shoulder, cracked open the door and then tried to push Santos through it.

"We have to hurry. Santos won't last much longer."

The woman saw Alex struggling to push a huge dog on a cart. She used the dead man's gun to prop the door open and pushed the dog to the SUV. She opened the back door and told Alex to get in. The lady pushed Santos to the back and opened the hatch. She grunted as her adrenaline gave her strength to transfer Santos from the cart to the SUV. She looked around before pushing the cart back to the tunnel door and down the tunnel. She placed the gun back on the dead man and she and Alex pulled off. She picked up her phone to find the nearest veterinarian office. It was ten miles away. As she drove, she looked in the rearview mirror at Alex sitting stone faced in the backseat. Alex's eyes met hers and she asked what her name was.

"Violet Jones."

CHAPTER 5

"Cleo, no one has seen the girl." Trig said from his end of the phone.

"She didn't just disappear. She is ten fucking years old." Cleo yelled back into the phone. "Watch your teeth bitch!" he said to the lady on her knees in front of him.

"We checked the house three times yesterday before we left, and I left three men at the perimeter near the roads. If she was there, we would have found her," Trig replied.

"Fuck! If one of you mother fuckers killed my daughter, I will kill all of you!" Cleo yelled.

"Man, chill the fuck out. She isn't here. For all we know Marko may have played both sides and got her out before we made it. Probably to ask for a ransom and shit." Trig reasoned.

Cleo thought for a moment and after putting his hands on the back the lady's head, he answered. "Yeah, you right. We need to find Marko and see where he put my daughter. I have big plans for her. We gonna run this shit together in few years. I ain't stopping until I find her."

"Bet." Trig hung up and texted his men to meet back at the spot. He knew that if they haven't found her yet, they weren't going to. He was sure that Marko took her.

Violet and Alex rode the rest of the way to the vet in silence. Violet pulled into the parking lot and turned to Alex. "Do you have a gun?" Alex nodded. "Good. Use it if you need to. I will be back." As Violet walked into the building, Alex took in her surroundings. She saw a car pull into the parking lot and park right next to them. She crouched down in the SUV as she watched. A woman got out of the driver's side and two children got out of the back with a cat in a carrier. Alex saw Violet and two young men walking towards the SUV. Alex put her gun in her bag and sat up. Violet opened the hatch and the two men lifted Santos in the blanket. Violet followed the men back into the building and returned to the SUV a few minutes later. She got in and looked in the back at Alex.

"You should have left the dog," she said.

Alex just stared at her but didn't respond.

Violet sighed. "I know you are hurting and that this is hard, but you should have left the dog. Your uncle should have told you that. You should have known that. We can't wait around for him. We have to go."

Alex's eyes went big with shock and then watered. "Please. I had to leave Uncle Frankie, I couldn't leave Santos, too."

Violet sighed again. "Ok. We will wait as long as we can, but if something pops off, you better put on your big girl panties and be ready to fight." Violet reached into the passenger's seat and opened a duffel bag. "Let's get a few things straight." She pulled out a folder and looked at the contents. "Your name is Avery Elaine Jones. Your date of birth is now August 17. I'm your aunt, and your mother and father, Eva and Jeff Jones died in a car accident in 2004, and it has been just the two of us since then. Jeff was my brother. You grew up in Shreveport, Louisiana, and we moved because of my job." Violet closed the folder.

"I know my back story," Alex responded softly. "I just didn't know your name."

"Good. Since you now know my name, you know everything. Now we need to cut your hair." Violet pulled out a pair of scissors from the bag. Alex turned around and let Violet snip off her ponytail. She placed the hair in a plastic bag and put it back in the black duffel bag. She handed Alex a brush.

Alex brushed her short curls down. Her once long, curly hair now barely covered her ears.

"You hungry?" Violet asked. Alex nodded her head yes. Violet handed her a protein bar and a cold bottle of water.

"Thank you." Alex whispered.

"No problem." Violet handed her another protein bar. "So, Avery, do you have any questions?"

Alex furrowed her brow for a moment before remembering that her name is now Avery. "Where are we going?"

"We are leaving California and going to a safe house that your uncle had set up for you in Virginia. If all goes well, we will stay there. If it doesn't, we will move on to another safe house. Your uncle really loved you and made sure that you would be taken care of whether he was alive or not." Violet swallowed hard on the last part of that sentence.

Alex sniffed before she answered. "How did you know my uncle? Were you his girlfriend?"

Violet laughed. "Oh, no, nothing like that. I grew up with Frankie and Juan. Frankie helped me out when I had no one else to turn to. No family, no anything. I owe him my life, and that's why I am who he trusted you with." Violet opened a bottle of water and took a big gulp before she asked her next question. "Who killed Frankie?"

"Cleo," Alex answered.

Violet stared at Alex before she asked. "Cleo?"

Alex nodded.

"What about Juan? Is he dead too?" Violet asked.

"I don't know. I haven't seen him." Alex answered honestly.

"Well, it's my job to protect you, and to teach you how to protect yourself when I am not around." Violet sat her water in the cup holder.

"I already know how to protect myself. My uncle taught me everything that I need to know." Alex responded with confidence.

"Good," Violet said. "I'm going to go and check on the dog."

"Can I come, too?" Alex pleaded.

"Yeah, come on." Violet stepped out of the SUV and looked around before grabbing Alex's hand. "If I tap your leg, you need to lay on the waterworks if you want to take this dog with us."

Alex nodded her head in agreement and walked hand and hand in the building with Violet. After sitting in the waiting area for an hour and a half, Violet was about to tell Alex that they had to go when the vet came out and asked to speak to them. He led them back to where Santos was. He was lying on the table, breathing better than he was when Violet first saw him, and had a bandage on his chest.

"You're lucky you got him here when you did, he was almost gone. We removed the bullet and gave him seven units of blood. He is going to be fine. We will keep an eye on him for the next four hours and then you can take him home. In about 24 hours he will be on his way to being as good as new. But let this big beast take it easy for the next week or so. He needs to heal. I am going to send you home with antibiotics and a few pain pills. Give him the pain pills as needed, but he may not even need them." The veterinarian bent down to speak to Alex. "Do you want to stay with him while I go speak to your mother?"

Violet discreetly tapped Alex on the leg and on cue Alex let the tears flow. Sobbing she said, "Yes, sir. I don't want to leave him."

"There, there, sweetie. Everything is going to be ok. You stay right here with him, ok." The veterinarian said to Alex. She nodded and rubbed Santos' head. He walked Violet to the front desk and spoke to her privately.

"You said that you guys found him on the property like that and that you think that your neighbors may have shot him?" he asked.

"Yes, sir. He has dug a hole under the fence and gotten out before and terrorized their chickens. It was our fault. My husband was supposed to fix the fence and he just hasn't had time to fix it yet, and well, you know. He was in this condition this morning when we found him. My little girl is so torn up about it." Violet lied smoothly.

"I suggest that you still file an incident report. I will need to see him again one week from today." The elderly gentleman smiled at Violet.

"Yes, sir. And we will leave here and go straight to file a report," Violet lied.

"Good. Michelle can check you out here. I will give your daughter a few more moments with her dog. You can just go back and get her when you are done." He patted Violet's shoulder and disappeared into the back of the building.

"Ok. Here are the antibiotics and pain pills. We need to schedule your follow up appointment for next week. Morning or afternoon?" Michelle asked.

"Morning is fine, thank you." Violet smiled innocently at Michelle as she put the pills in her pocket.

"Ok." Michelle wrote the appointment date and time on the card and then handed it to Violet. "Your total today is $668.92. You can come back around seven tonight to pick up Buddy. You will just drive around the back and pick him up. That's where we do our after-hours pick up."

Violet patted her pockets. "I left my wallet in the truck. I will be right back." Violet exited the building and looked around before heading to her SUV. She drove around to the back exit and then walked back inside through the front door. She handed the lady $680.00 and waited for her change. "I'm going to go to the back and get my daughter and we will see you guys around seven." Violet walked to the back where Santos and Alex were. She unlocked the wheels on the table Santos was on and told Alex to open the back door. She wheeled Santos out of the building and to the back of her SUV, carefully loading him in. Violet pushed the table back to its position in the room and then she and Alex walked hand and hand through the building, waved goodbye to Michelle and then walked back to the SUV and got in. Violet eased out of the parking lot, starting their journey to Virginia.

"Thank you." Alex said.

"Yeah." Violet said. "It's gonna take us a minimum of three days to get to where we are going. You might as well get comfortable back there. We will stay in cash only motels along the way and eat only fast food. We have to make sure we aren't being followed."

"Yes, ma'am." Alex said as she watched Santos sleep. "What's your real name?"

"All you need to know is Violet Jones," Violet said as she continued to drive.

"Yes, ma'am." Alex said.

Violet looked at Alex in the mirror. She was a beautiful little girl, but Violet thought to herself that it is too bad that she had to grow up so fast. She knew that was the one thing that Frankie didn't want. Eight hours and three stops later, Violet pulled into the motel. After getting the keycard, Violet entered the room first, checking under the beds and in the bathroom. She walked back to the SUV and told Alex to get her bag and come on. Santos slowly got out of the SUV and followed Alex into the room.

"You need to take him outside and let him do his business," Violet said to Alex.

"Yes, ma'am," Alex said. She, Santos, and Violet walked to the grassy area and Santos used the bathroom and then sat at Alex's feet. "Good boy!" Alex rubbed his head, and he wagged his tail.

Back in the motel room, they got ready for bed. When Alex went into the bathroom, Santos waited outside the door for her. When she got into the bed, he sat on the floor next to her. Violet watched Santos and Alex. She saw why Alex couldn't leave him behind. Alex would never have made it without him.

"So, this is where we are." Violet said. "You have a birth certificate and passport stating that you are Avery Elaine Jones, Alexandria

Pena is gone. Your uncle also has a trust fund set up for you in that name, and he has left you enough cash on hand to get whatever you need. When we get to where we are going, I will enroll you in school. You will be in public school now." Violet tried to gauge her reaction. She didn't flinch. "From now on it's just me and you. No guards, and no one looking out for us. We have to protect ourselves."

"What will happen to me if something happens to you?" Avery asked.

"Nothing is going to happen to me," Violet said as she stood to check the locks on the door before going to the bathroom.

"But what if it does?" Avery sat up in the bed.

"Then there is another plan, someone else to take care of you," Violet lied.

"Oh." Avery's eyes watered, but no tears fell.

Violet shut the bathroom door behind her, turned on the shower, and then closed the lid on the toilet. She sat on the toilet and cried silently. She couldn't believe that Frankie was gone. Her Frankie was dead, and now she had a little girl that she had to protect. Violet cried until she had nothing left. After she showered, she got into bed and looked at a sleeping Avery. She knew that no matter what she had to keep her safe. Violet closed her eyes and sleep came easily.

CHAPTER 6

||||||||||||||||||||||||||||||||||||||||||||||||||||||||||||||||||||||||||||||||||||||

After three days, they made it to Virginia. Violet entered the code at the gate and went through it. As they pulled into the driveway, Avery took notice of the security features. There was a wireless driveway alarm, security cameras at the entrance of the driveway and on each corner of the house. There was a camera at the front door as well. The cameras were small and undetectable to the untrained eye. Violet hit the garage opener and pulled in. The three of them entered the house through the mudroom. Santos sniffed around the house while Avery walked around, taking in everything. She knocked on the sides of the kitchen island as she walked around it. She heard the hollowness of one side and pushed against the edge. The false side opened. Violet went to the knife block and selected a knife. She watched as Avery observed and touched everything. She walked up behind Avery and went to stab her in the back. Avery turned, grabbed her wrist, knocked the knife away, and hit Violet with a quick strike to the throat. Violet gasped for air. Once she caught her breath she smiled.

"Frankie has done a great job with you." She grabbed Avery's hand. "Let me show you everything that you need to know."

"Do you live here?" Avery asked.

"Yep." Violet kept walking until she reached a door. "This is your room." Avery walked in and smiled. It was a replica of her room back in California, only smaller. She placed her bag on the bed and went to her bookshelf. It was a lot smaller than the one at home, but it had her secret compartment with a compact .22 in it. She smiled. She went to the mirror that hung on the wall and slid it to the right. The concealed door behind it opened, revealing a corridor to what Avery assumed was the basement. "It's just like home." She said as she smiled at Violet. Violet smiled back. Avery looked in her closet that was already filled with clothes in her size. She walked back into her room when something on the dresser caught her eye. She picked up. It was a necklace with a heart locket on it. She opened the locket and there was a picture of her Uncle Frankie in it. She closed the locket and started to cry. Santos sat at her feet whimpering. Violet held back her own tears as she watched Avery cry. When her cries turned into wails of sorrow, Violet comforted her.

"Shhh. It's going to be ok. We will get through this together. Lo prometo." Violet said.

"Hablas espanol?" Avery asked.

"Si, chica." Violet ran her hands through Avery's short curls. "I know that he loved you very much and that you were his heart."

"Will you help me with the necklace, Aunt Violet?" Avery asked.

"I sure will. Turn around." Violet clasped the necklace around Avery's neck. "Now he will always be with you."

"Siempre. Always," Avery said as she held the heart in her hand.

"Why don't I show you the rest of the house tomorrow? You can take a bath and then go to bed if you like," Violet said.

"I'm ok. I want to see the rest of the house." Avery hopped off the bed and she and Santos followed Violet around the house. Before she went to bed, she knew all the secret rooms, weapons, where the tunnel was, and the codes to the gate, the VPN internet connection, and the alarm. Avery got on her knees to say her prayers before she got into bed. Avery and Santos were so tired that they didn't wake up until noon the following day. Avery found Violet in the kitchen on her laptop.

"Good morning, sleepy head. Well, good afternoon." Violet stood and went to the fridge. "Do you want an omelet?"

"Yes, ma'am. I need to take Santos outside first. I'm sure he needs to go." Avery said.

"Ok. Well, I will get started on your omelet." Violet started taking the ingredients out of the fridge.

"Ok." Avery went to put on her shoes and got her gun. She used the back door to walk Santos to the back of the property, away from the house. She checked her surroundings as he sniffed and relieved himself. When they made it back inside, she sat at the island and placed her gun in front of her. Violet laughed.

"We don't have armed guards, but you can still walk outside safely." Violet laughed again. "We have two gates, and we will be alerted if someone gets over the first one or if anyone even gets close to the house. You are safe here inside and out."

Avery smiled at Violet. "Ok."

"But I like the way that you think." She reached into a kitchen drawer and handed Avery a pocketknife. "Here. This should be a little easier to carry."

"Thank you," Avery said as she waited for her omelet. Violet placed the plate in front of her and she dug in.

"So, I figure we can enroll you in school on Monday," Violet said.

Avery shrugged and kept eating her omelet.

"We also need to go to the store and get some groceries and dog food. This beast can really eat." Violet fed Santos a strip of bacon. Avery giggled as he licked Violet's fingers.

"He likes you. He usually doesn't like strangers." Avery patted her leg and Santos walked over to her and sat at her feet.

"He is healing nicely," Violet said. She looked at her laptop and shook her head.

"What?" Avery asked.

Violet wiped a tear from her eye. "I was looking up Frankie online, and nothing came up."

"Is that a good thing?" The hope in Avery's voice was evident.

Violet shook her head. "No, it's not. That means that the cleaners did their job. That man always was a step ahead." She let out a heavy breath.

"What about my old school? Won't they wonder where I am?" Avery finished her omelet and put her plate in fork in the dishwasher.

"No, your uncle has already taken care of that as well. Once the lawyer gets your records, it will be like you never existed." Violet turned off her laptop.

"Aunt Violet, what do you know about my dad?" Avery asked.

"Well, what do you know about him?" Violet countered.

Avery took a deep breath. "Nothing. My Uncle Frankie never talked about him, but I know that Cleo called me his daughter before he shot and killed my Uncle Frankie. And I know that as soon as I get older, I am going to find him and kill him."

"What else did he say?" She asked.

"He asked where I was and said that he loved my mother. He also said that Uncle Frankie killed his son and brother and tried to kill him," Avery explained. She popped the blade on the knife and started twirling it between her fingers.

"Frankie was an honorable man. He loved and protected his family fiercely. He loved your mother. She used to follow him around and wanted to be just like him. He would do anything for her. Frankie warned her about Cleo. He told her that Cleo was nothing but a thug, and that she shouldn't get involved with him. She didn't listen. Frankie did what he had to do to keep her safe. To keep you safe." Violet watched as Avery continued twirling the knife in her hands. Frankie raised her to be killer, and it showed.

"That man took away the only family I had. Uncle Frankie was the only person that I had to love me, and now he is gone. Cleo is not my father, he is my enemy, and I will kill him." Avery closed the blade and placed the knife on the countertop.

"You have plenty of time to plot your revenge, but for right now, let's get dressed and pick up a few items at the store." Violet tried to change the subject. Her heart broke for Avery. She knew that carrying around hatred in your heart was a burden that many were ill prepared to carry.

"Did you love my Uncle Frankie? I heard you crying that first night at the hotel," Avery asked.

Violet stopped in her tracks and turned to face Avery. "Yes. I loved him very much. I want Cleo dead as much as you do, but you are a ten-year-old and you should act like one. Frankie taught you what he did to keep you alive, not for you to go tracking down and killing people."

"But-"

"No buts. We will continue to train like Frankie trained you, but you need to let it go now. Frankie is gone, and he is never coming back. You go chasing after Cleo and you will be next!" Violet raised her voice as she spoke.

Violet saw something flash in Avery's eyes, and it scared her. It was the same look of determination that Frankie had when he made up his mind about something. The same look of all fearlessness leaving and being replaced by hatred and revenge. Avery pasted a smile on her face and said, "Yes, ma'am." Then she walked into her room to get dressed. Violet stood there stunned at how much Avery was like Frankie. "Frankie, what in the hell have you gotten me into?" Violet said aloud and laughed as she picked up the knife from the countertop and took it to Avery. She opened Avery's bedroom door and tossed her the knife.

"You forgot this kiddo."

Avery caught the knife with her right hand and placed it in her pocket. "Thanks Aunt Vy."

They walked through the grocery store picking up items that they needed. Avery picked up Santos some treats and a new black collar. They went aisle by aisle picking assorted items and placing them in the shopping cart.

"Hey, you want some chocolate? Or some of these? I used to love this candy when I was your age." Violet held up a bag of taffy.

"No, Uncle-" Avery stopped herself. "I don't really eat much candy or sweets. It's not good for you," she said.

"Oh. Well, I will get these for myself." Violet put the bag of candy in the shopping cart. "What about chips, you want some chips?"

"Um, no, not really," Avery said, disinterested in everything around her. She only had revenge on her mind.

Violet stopped the cart and looked at Avery. "Hey, I know that this is hard for you, it is hard for me, too, but it's going to be ok. I promise." She walked back down the aisle to the chocolate and picked up a chocolate bar for Avery and put it in the cart. "One chocolate bar won't hurt."

"The last time I went to the movies I could get whatever I wanted. I got a chocolate bar, nachos with cheese and extra peppers, popcorn, and a drink. And we went out for ice cream afterwards. I had the best day ever." Avery smiled and reached for the locket she wore around her neck.

"So, you like to go to the movies?" Violet asked.

"Yeah, I do," she said. "I can't believe he let me get all those things. And I ate it all and it was such a good movie." Avery said as they walked down the next aisle.

They continued talking and bonding as they shopped in the store. The more Violet listened, the more she realized how special the bond was between Avery and Frankie. While Avery was raised privileged and got most of what she asked for, she wasn't spoiled or bratty. She respected everyone, and under all that dangerous demeanor, she was just a little ten-year-old girl. Avery helped to unload the groceries and put them away. For dinner they had baked chicken and rice with a salad. After dinner, Violet touched up Avery's haircut and made it a cute pixie cut.

"Do you want me to straighten your hair for you?" Violet asked.

Avery looked in the mirror and ran her fingers through her hair. "No, thanks. I like my curls. My Uncle Frankie said that they are just like my mother's."

"They are. In fact, you look like her," Violet said.

"Why do you straighten your hair?" Avery asked.

"I like it straight," Violet shrugged.

"I think it is prettier curly." Avery hopped out of the chair. "I'm going to take a bath and go to bed now. Thank you for fixing my hair." Avery hugged Violet tight. "Goodnight, Aunt Violet."

Violet rested her chin on the top of Avery's head. "Goodnight, sweet girl."

CHAPTER 7

||||||||||||||||||||||||||||||||||||||||||||||||||||||||||||||||||||||||||||||||||||

"Call me if you need me, ok?" Violet said.

"Yes, ma'am, I will." Avery hugged Violet and then followed the principal to her new classroom.

"Alright, Avery. This is the fifth-grade hall, and this will be your homeroom class. This is Mrs. Smith. Mrs. Smith, this is your new student, Avery Jones. She just moved here from Louisiana." Principal Tucker introduced Avery to a homely looking middle-aged white woman that wore gold wire rimmed glasses and had brown hair that reached her butt.

"Good morning, Avery. Go ahead and have a seat. We were about to go over our math homework." Mrs. Smith smiled at Avery. Avery nodded and took the empty seat in the back of the class. She sat behind a Hispanic girl. The girl turned around and whispered to Avery.

"Hi, I'm Tonya. I like your haircut. It's cute." Tonya smiled at Avery.

"Thanks." Avery smiled back and took out her pencil and paper.

"Ok, guys. Let's start with number one. Avery, follow along as best you can. We are doing order of operations." Mrs. Smith wrote the problem on the board. "Who would like to come to the board and solve it?" She looked around the class and no one raised their hand. "Come on guys, I know that someone can solve it."

Avery looked around at her classmates before raising her hand.

"Oh, well, ok. You are more than welcomed to try it out." Mrs. Smith handed Avery the dry erase marker.

Avery worked the problem on the board, handed the marker back to Mrs. Smith, and took her seat at the back of the class.

"That is correct, Avery. Good job. Let's go step by step and see how she came up with her answer." As Mrs. Smith explained how to work the problem, Avery saw a blonde headed girl whisper something to the black girl next to her and they both looked at Avery and snickered. Tonya turned around to Avery and said, "Don't worry about Emma. She is a bully." Avery nodded and continued to watch as Mrs. Smith worked the remaining problems on the board.

At recess, Avery walked the track by herself. Emma walked by with a group of girls and bumped into Avery. "Oops. My bad." Emma said as she flipped her blonde hair over her shoulder. She and the other girls in the group laughed and kept walking. Tonya, another Hispanic girl, and a black girl caught up to Avery.

"Emma is such a witch. Do you want me to tell Coach Davis on her?" Tonya asked Avery.

"No, it's ok. I'm not worried about Emma." Avery kept walking.

"You can walk with us if you want to," Tonya said.

"Ok." Avery walked with the girls and listened as they talked about everything from the upcoming social studies test to the new show on Nickelodeon. When Coach Davis blew her whistle, they all lined back up to go inside.

The day went by slowly, and so far, no one had even talked to Avery except Tonya. During lunch, she took the empty seat next to her classmate that was autistic. He asked Avery if she would help him open his pudding, and she opened it for him. As she ate her lunch that Aunt Violet packed, she looked up when she saw Emma take the seat in front of her. Avery continued to eat her lunch like Emma didn't even exist.

Emma threw an English pea at Avery. Avery flicked the pea off the table and continued eating her sandwich. Emma flicked another pea at Avery. Avery put her sandwich down on the table and looked at Emma. "Do you have a problem?"

"Yeah, I do, you. You think you are so smart and so cute, don't you?" Emma countered back.

"I don't think anything," Avery said.

Emma rolled her eyes and stuck her finger in her mouth and then put it through Avery's sandwich. "Oops. I hope you weren't gonna finish that."

Avery's went to grab Emma's hand but stopped herself. She put her sandwich back into the sandwich bag and looked at Emma. "No, I was done with it." Avery said.

Emma laughed and moved to the other end of the table next to her friends.

"She is mean," her classmate said to her.

"Yes, she is, but I am ok. You tell me if she is ever mean to you, ok," Avery said.

"Ok. Will you be my friend?" he asked.

"I sure will. My name is Avery. What's your name?" Avery asked.

"My name is Brad," he said.

"Nice to meet you, Brad," Avery said as she finished her water and packed up her lunchbox.

When Violet picked up Avery from school, she asked how her first day was.

"It was ok. I already know the stuff that they are going over now, so it's easy," Avery said.

"Well, did you make any friends?" Violet asked.

"Yeah, two. Tonya and Brad."

"Look at you, making friends. That's great." Violet merged into traffic.

"Yeah." Avery said as she looked out of the window on the ride home.

When they made it home, Avery and Santos went in her room, and she shut the door. Violet decided not to bother her and let her have some alone time. After their round of boxing, and dinner, they played a game of monopoly before going to bed. Tuesday morning, when Violet made it to the basement, Avery was already on the treadmill. She looked at the dashboard and saw that she was on her second mile.

"Impressive. It's only five o'clock." Violet started stretching and looked over at Avery. "You know we could start running outside if you want to. We have two acres. We could run the perimeter."

Avery slowed the treadmill down before stopping it and started doing her pushups, not saying a word. After her pushups she went to her sit ups, never missing a beat. Violet shrugged and waited for her to stop.

"Do you want to spar this morning?" Violet asked. Avery nodded and took her stance. Violet nodded, and Avery charged at her. Avery went to strike her in the stomach, but Violet caught her hand, twisting it behind her back, while wrapping her other arm around Avery's neck.

"Calm down," she said as she pushed Avery down on the basement floor. Avery got up and charged her again, landing a blow to her chest. Violet recovered quickly, and swept her leg under Avery, knocking her to the floor and stopping just short of striking her in the face. "I said calm down! You can't fight and win when you are emotional."

Avery pushed away both of Violet's arms and got on her feet. She went to kick Violet, but Violet blocked it, she punched right, left, and right again. Violet blocked the punches and jabbed her in the side. The blow knocked Avery to the ground again. She got up in tears and ran up the basement stairs and to her room.

"Shit," Violet said as she followed Avery up the stairs. "Wait. Avery. Wait."

She found Avery lying across her bed crying. "Why did he have to die and leave me? Why! It was supposed to be me and him forever and he left me!"

"Shhh. No, honey, he didn't leave you. You know that your Uncle Frankie would do anything for you and if he could still be with you, he would be. You were the best part of his life." Violet rubbed Avery's back as she cried.

"Who's gonna love me now? He was the only family I had. I don't have anyone now." Avery's sobs made Santos whimper.

Violet swallowed the lump in her throat, fighting back tears. "I miss your Uncle Frankie, too. You have me, Avery. We are a family now."

"We're not a real family! My uncle probably just paid you to take care of me. You don't love me." Avery cried even harder.

Violet didn't respond. What could she say? She rubbed Avery's back until her cries stopped. "Do you want to stay home today from school?"

Avery shook her head. "No, I will be fine." Avery hopped off the bed and went into the bathroom to shower.

Violet sighed and ran her fingers through her hair. She left Avery's room and went into the kitchen to make breakfast and Avery's lunch.

"Have a good day at school, ok. Call me if you need me," Violet said.

"Ok." Avery shut the car door and headed to her homeroom classroom.

The day went the same as the day before. At recess, she did meet some more students from the other classes that were nice to her.

"Are you mixed with something? Girl, you got all this good hair," Janeice said to her at recess.

"No, I'm not," Avery lied.

"Well, you have some pretty hair," Janeice said.

"Thanks," Avery said as it was her turn to kick in kick ball. She kicked it as hard as she could and ran as fast as she could. She made it all the way home. Her teammates high fived her as she took her place at the end of the line.

"Good job, Avery." Tonya hugged her. "You have to be on my team every time."

Avery smiled.

At lunch, Avery sat next to Brad again. He offered to split his fruit snacks with Avery, but she told him no thank you. Tonya and Alicia sat across from them.

"Por que se sienta a lado del retrasado?" Alicia said to Tonya.

Avery shot her a look. "He isn't retarded, and I can sit wherever I please."

Alicia and Tonya sat there in shock. "You speak Spanish?" Alicia asked.

"Yeah, and the next time you call him out of his name or refer to him in that way, we will have a problem. His name is Brad," Avery said. Brad was oblivious to the conversation happening beside him, instead he was focused on eating his goldfish crackers.

"Ok," Alicia said and continued eating her lunch.

After school, Tonya caught up with Avery. "Hey, Av, wait up."

Avery slowed down and waited on Tonya to catch up to her.

"You know that Alicia wasn't trying to be mean," Tonya said.

"Maybe not, but it was rude and mean." Avery kept walking to the car rider line.

"Why didn't you tell me you speak Spanish?" Tonya asked.

"Why does it matter?" Avery countered back.

"I mean, not many black kids speak Spanish, is all," Tonya said. "I think it is pretty cool how you took up for Brad today though. He doesn't have many friends."

"Yeah," was Avery's response.

"Well, there's my dad. I will see you tomorrow." Tonya waved goodbye as she got into the minivan.

"See you tomorrow," Avery echoed as she got into the back of Violet's SUV and shut the door.

"How was school?" Violet asked.

"It was ok," Avery said. "I'm sorry about what I said this morning, I was just upset."

"No problem. We both have some adjusting to do. So, what do you say we go to the movies to catch a matinee?" Violet asked.

Avery couldn't keep the smile off her face. "Really?"

"Yes, really. You deserve a movie. And popcorn and nachos and candy and a drink." Violet winked at Avery, and she laughed.

"Yes!" Avery buckled her seatbelt as they headed to the movie theater.

"That was a good movie! The mummy was so cool!" Avery said as she got into the backseat.

"I thought that it was good, too. Mummies coming alive. Very cool," Violet said.

"Yes, it was. Can we have pizza tonight?" Avery asked.

"You read my mind. We will get a pizza and take it home. I know you have homework to do." Violet pulled off and drove towards the pizza parlor. She looked in the rearview mirror and noticed a black car with dark tinted windows tailing her a little too close for comfort. She reached in the arm rest, retrieved her gun, and sat it in her lap. She made a right turn and the black car turned right behind her. She took the next right and so did the black car. She took the third right and the car did the same. She made the fourth right, but the black car kept going straight. She silently released the breath she was holding.

"Good thing that car wasn't following us," Avery said.

"Why do you say that?" Violet asked.

"Because you took four rights. That takes you back to where you started and that's how you know if someone is following you." Avery put a handful of leftover popcorn in her mouth.

"You are exactly right." Violet was impressed by Avery's street sense.

"Besides, they looked like a bunch of kids smoking some weed," Avery said so matter of fact.

"Well, looks can be deceiving. Look at you. You're just a kid and you could kill a grown man if you had to." Violet turned into the restaurant's parking lot.

"True," Avery added as she jumped out of the SUV and wiped her hands on the front of her jeans.

"Pepperoni and mushroom, right?" Violet asked.

"Right," Avery echoed.

After making it home, finishing homework and dinner, they said their goodnights and Avery got ready for bed. After saying her prayers, she and Santos got into bed.

"Goodnight, Santos. I love you." Avery hugged Santos tight. He licked her face and walked to the foot of her king-sized bed.

"A dormir, a dormir, a dormir, mi bebito." Avery yawned as she sang the lullaby that Uncle Frankie had sung her since as long as she could remember.

"Que tus suenos sean siempre. De more, carino y paz." Violet finished the lullaby in a whisper as she leaned against the wall outside of Avery's room. She held onto the locket that she wore around her neck that also held a picture of Frankie. She stood outside of Avery's room until she fell asleep before returning to her bedroom.

CHAPTER 8

||||||||||||||||||||||||||||||||||||||||||||||||||||||||||||||||||||||||||||||||||||||

A very had been in school for a month, and she was settling in very well. She had made a few friends and had aced all her tests and assignments. She started to feel like she belonged somewhere and was safe. She washed her hands after using the restroom and pulled off a paper towel from the paper towel holder to dry her hands. As she opened the door to leave the bathroom, Emma walked in.

"Where do you think you are going you little lesbian?" She pushed Avery down on the floor.

Avery got up and balled up her fists at her sides and then relaxed them. She shook her head and went to walk around Emma, but she blocked her path.

"I know that you are a lesbian. That short hair and always hanging around Tonya and that special kid, Brad. How pathetic." Emma laughed.

Avery's anger rose to an uncontrollable level as she watched Emma laugh at her. She took two deep, calming breaths and smiled. "Emma, I am not a lesbian, and you are right about me hanging around with Tonya and Brad. They are both my friends, and Brad is pretty special to me. So, let's get one thing straight." Avery stood toe to toe with

Emma. Avery was five foot two, so she suspected that Emma was about two inches taller than she was, about the same height as Violet. She looked Emma up and down before she spoke. "I don't like bullies, and I don't like that you are mean to people for no reason. You are a bully, and if you put another hand on me, I will break it."

"Try it," Emma replied and went to push Avery again.

Avery caught her arm and twisted it around her back, pushing Emma against the wall. She twisted her hand until Emma squealed, then loosened her grip, before letting her go. "Leave me alone. Leave Tonya alone, and leave Brad alone. In fact, if you don't have anything nice to say, don't say anything at all. Try being nice and see how good it makes you feel." Emma held back her tears as she rubbed her arm and twisted her sore wrist. "See you in class." Avery turned and walked out of the bathroom, leaving a stunned Emma standing against the wall. Avery half expected to be called into the principal's office before the day was out, but the call never came. She figured that Emma didn't want to admit to being handled by the new girl, so she kept her mouth shut. Besides, Avery made sure not to hurt her too bad or break anything. From that day on, Emma made it her business to go the opposite direction of Avery, and she stopped being a bully and started being nice. She even invited Avery to her 11th birthday party, but Avery didn't go.

Summer turned into fall and fall to winter. For Christmas, Avery didn't ask for anything. The one thing that she wanted she couldn't have, so she decided that she wouldn't ask for anything at all. It was her first Christmas without her Uncle Frankie, and it was hard for her. She bought Violet a sweater and scarf, and Violet bought her a new pair of boots and a diary. There was one gift left under the tree and Avery looked at it. It was for her from Violet. She opened the gift and immediately started crying. It was a framed picture of Avery and Frankie that was taken about a year ago.

"Thank you so much!" Avery hugged Violet tight. "I love it!" She wiped her tears away. "Where did you get it from?" she asked.

"Every year I received a picture of you so that I knew what you looked like if the time ever came that I would have to come get you." Violet's voice cracked. She still got choked up when thought about Frankie. "I found it, and I knew that you would like it."

"Like it, I love it! Thank you again. I love you so much!" Avery threw her arms around Violet again.

Violet was stunned at Avery's admission that she loved her. They were a family, but they never told each other that they loved one another. She wrapped her arms around Avery and hugged her back. "I love you, too, Avery."

They held that position for a few moments until Avery broke the hug to look at the picture. She remembered taking that picture. They had just finished swimming in the pool and then started throwing balls into the pool for Santos to fetch. She ran her fingers across his face. She could still remember every line on his face, his laugh, his smell, his hugs, and his voice.

I love you, my heart.

"I love you, too, Uncle Frankie," Avery said to herself. She excused herself to her room and placed the picture on her nightstand beside her bed. She laid across the bed and stared at the picture. She looked up when she heard the knock on her door.

"Hey, you ready for breakfast? Santos is." Violet said as Santos stood and looked at Avery.

She laughed. "Yeah, we are both ready for breakfast."

That Christmas turned out to be better than they both expected. They both realized that they loved and needed each other, and they were a real family now.

Avery threw her things into the back of the SUV like she did every afternoon after school and climbed in the front seat.

"Aunt Violet don't forget that track tryouts start tomorrow after school, so you won't have to pick me up until 5 every day," Avery said.

"Well, hey to you, too," Violet said sarcastically.

"I'm sorry, Aunt Vy. Hey, how was your day?" Avery leaned across the seat and kissed her aunt on the cheek.

"It was good, baby, thanks for asking. Are you feeling confident about taking your permit test today?" Violet merged into traffic.

"Yes, ma'am." Avery pulled out her phone and started listening to music like the typical fifteen-year-old she was.

Five years had passed since Avery lost her Uncle Frankie and gained an Aunt Violet. They waited day after day, year after year, for any sign of Cleo or his men, and none came. Violet and Avery were always aware that a threat could come at any time, so they continued to train everyday like usual, upping the ante and becoming more physical, and shooting heavier guns. Avery now stood at 5'7", so Violet had up her game against the fifteen-year-old, now that she was taller, and Violet was 37 years old. She would be the first to admit that Avery kept her young.

"I know I have to get my permit first, but when I pass my driver's test, can I get a car?" Avery asked.

"Yeah, your uncle already had one on order for you. A black, bulletproof, four door crossover SUV," Violet answered.

"Sweet!" Avery smiled.

"Yeah, but same rules still apply. You must keep all A's, you can't have anyone ride with you unless I know about it, and I need to know where you are at all times," Violet said sternly as she turned off the car.

"Yes, ma'am." Avery unbuckled her seatbelt.

"Ok, now go ahead and pass that test." Violet kissed Avery on her cheek. Avery smiled and walked inside the building to take her permit test.

Twenty minutes later she came out with a small piece of paper and a smile

"I passed!" she said as she climbed into the SUV.

"Great job, baby." Violet hugged her. "Now, Lord help us all," she said as she drove home.

Avery laughed. "I can't wait for the hard copy of my permit. I took a good picture, too."

"I will say that the short hair looks good on you. I thought that you would want to grow it back out by now," Violet commented.

"Nah, I like it short. It's better for running, too." Avery said.

"Well, I'm very proud of the young lady you have become. You are beautiful inside and out, and Frankie would be so proud of you," Violet said.

"I think he would, too." Avery subconsciously reached for her necklace and held it tight. "While we are giving out compliments, I am glad that you started wearing your curls. It brings out your natural beauty. Senora muy bonita," Avery said to make Violet laugh. "My uncle always did like the pretty ladies."

Violet's smile faded for a second before it returned. "Yeah, he did."

Opening the door and greeting a waiting Santos, Violet told Avery that dinner would be ready by 7:30.

"Yes, ma'am. I am going to let Santos out and then start my homework. Come on boy." Santos trotted out the door with Avery. He may have gotten older, but he was still as playful as a puppy. He sniffed in his normal spots where he relieved himself while Avery watched. They both looked to the right as a noise near the fence caught their attention. Avery instinctively reached for her pocketknife as Santos started growling. He charged, and Avery watched to see where he was going. He chased two squirrels across the yard and over the fence. Avery laughed and called him back into the house. After dinner, Avery wanted to get in some target practice. She placed her guns on the table in front of her like she always did and hung up her targets. She prepared herself to shoot, hearing her uncle's voice like she did every time she got ready to shoot.

Center mass. Go. Head shots. Go.

Every time she pulled the trigger, she heard her uncle's instructions, following them like she did since she first held a gun in her hand at six years old. She finished her target practice, showered, and went to bed.

Avery was a bundle of nerves before tryouts, but she felt like she had a good chance at making the team. She was the fastest girl in school, but she loved the long run. She really wanted to do cross country but would do whatever the coach needed her to. She was good at everything, but cross country was her passion.

"Yay, Avery!" Brad held up a sign and cheered for her along with Tonya and Alicia.

Avery smiled and waved to her cheering friends. This was the final day of tryouts, and a chance to show the coach what she was made of. She ran as fast and as hard as she could. After tryouts concluded, Coach Johnson said that he would post the list online by 7 that night. Everyone grabbed their things and wished each other luck. Avery made her way over to her three friends.

"Thanks, you guys for staying afterschool to watch." Avery hugged all three of them.

"No problem, chica," Tonya said. "You are like the best one out there, we know you made the team."

"Yeah, you did good, Avery," Brad said.

"And Greg out there looking fine. I should have tried out, too," Alicia said, looking thirstily at Greg.

"Is that all you think about?" Avery laughed at her friend.

"Mostly." She laughed.

They made their way to the parking lot.

"You guys want to go and get some pizza and wait for the results with me and Aunt Vy?" Avery asked.

"My mom is here. I have to go. We are having dinner with my grandma," Brad said.

Avery looked and waved at Mrs. Hillman, and she waved back. "Ok, Brad. I will see you Monday." She gave Brad a hug before he left.

"Sorry, chica, we are going to the movies tonight with Tony and Mike and doing a little something something afterwards," Tonya said.

"Alright, with y'all's fast behinds. Don't get pregnant," Avery said. They both laughed.

"No, seriously, don't get pregnant. And definitely don't catch a STD or STI. The rates are alarming. Make sure you guys use protection," Avery warned.

"Alright, Dr. Jones. We will be careful," Tonya said.

"Yeah, Madre, will be will careful," Alicia seconded. They hugged their friend and then got into Alicia's car and sped out of the parking lot.

Avery shook her head as she crossed the parking lot to a waiting Violet.

"So, how did it go?" Violet asked.

"I think it went very well. He will post who made the team by 7 tonight," Avery said.

"Great. Do you still want to get some pizza while we wait it out?" Violet asked.

"Yep," Avery answered, closing the back door.

"Ok. You drive. I want to finish this book." Violet held up her book.

"Ok." Avery smiled and walked to the driver's side and got in. She buckled up, adjusted her mirrors and seat, and then pulled out of the parking lot.

Violet had been letting Avery drive every now and then since she was twelve, so Avery was already comfortable behind the wheel.

Eating her favorite pepperoni and mushroom pizza, Avery pulled up the school's website and clicked on the link to the track team. She scrolled down and saw on her name on the list.

"Yes! I made the team. Yes!" Avery did a little dance in her seat.

Violet beamed with pride. "I knew that you would!"

"I have to text Brad, Tonya, and Alicia." Avery texted everyone and smiled as she read her congratulations texts. "Wow. I'm so excited."

"As you should be. We should cut back on the pizza and eat more fruits and veggies." Violet teased as she finished off her slice of pizza.

"Well, maybe we can order a veggie pizza." Avery laughed. "Aunt Vy, do you think that my mom would be proud of me?"

"Sweetie, there is no question about it, she would be very proud of you. You're a straight A student, you're a bright, beautiful, respectful young lady, and you are going to be a doctor one day. Of course, she would be proud of you." Violet smiled at Avery.

Avery smiled back at her aunt and wished that her uncle could be there with her.

"Come on, Avery, we are at the home stretch. You can do it. You can do it." Avery gave herself a pep talk as she entered the home stretch in the cross-country event of the track meet. When she heard the cheers from the crowd, she increased her pace and gave it her all until she made it to the finish line.

"Yeah, Avery!" She heard her teammates yell. She smiled as she looked in the bleachers for her Aunt Violet. She was on the front row cheering the hardest. Avery smiled as she realized that this was the first time that she saw her aunt genuinely happy. It seemed that in that moment, she forgot about the pressure and responsibility that she had taken on for the last five years, and she could just be happy.

That track meet was just the first of many that Avery would come first place in. Every track meet that she had, her Aunt Violet was there to cheer her on. Avery made the team her junior and senior year of school as well.

"Avery Elaine Jones." The principal called Avery's name.

Violet stood up and cheered, as well as Brad, Tonya, and Alicia as Avery walked across the stage to receive her high school diploma as class valedictorian. She participated in the dual enrollment program, so she would enter college as a sophomore.

"I'm so proud of you, honey." Violet wiped away her tears.

"Aunt Vy, don't cry," Avery said as she hugged her tight.

"I can't help it. I'm just so proud of you." She kissed Avery on her cheek. "Soon I will be calling you Dr. Jones."

"At your service," Avery said. She hugged her aunt one more time and then went to find her friends. After the graduation she went with her aunt to eat dinner.

"You didn't want to go out with your friends?" Violet asked.

"No, ma'am. I would rather be here with you and spend all the time I can with you these next few weeks." She said.

Violet's heart was full. "I appreciate it. I wish that you would have waited until the fall to start college instead of starting in the summer," Violet said honestly.

"You know that I want to go ahead and get it over with so I can start med school." Avery said.

"You are so ambitious and determined. I will never be able to put into words how proud I am of you. I love you, sweet pea," Violet said.

"I love you, too, Aunt Vy," Avery replied.

CHAPTER 9

||||||||||||||||||||||||||||||||||||||||||||||||||||||||||||||||||||||||||||||||

"Well, you are all set up. I guess I will head back home." Violet stood and picked up her purse. "You know all of the codes and you have your gun and knives, right?" she asked.

"Yes, ma'am, I have them. You have the extra key, right?" Avery questioned.

Violet picked up her keyring and showed the apartment key to Avery. "Got it. You have a landline and your cell phone. We have the VPN connection set up. You have Santos' leash and dog bed. I am gonna miss that old beast." Santos trotted over to Violet and sat at her feet. Violet reached down and rubbed Santos' head and let him give her a kiss on her cheek. "And I'm going to miss you." She pulled Avery into a hug. "Call me if you need me. Anytime. Day or night. And I expect a call or text every day. Even if it is just to say hey."

"Yes, ma'am. Every day. We will be fine. I will be careful, I promise."

"I know you will. I'm just gonna miss you. I love you. I better go before I start crying." Violet said as she headed towards the door.

"Bye, Aunt Violet. I love you, too." Avery walked her to the door, hugging and kissing her goodbye before shutting and locking it behind her. She walked into her bedroom in her apartment and looked at the picture of her and Uncle Frankie. "Well, Uncle Frankie, we did it. In a few more years, I will be the doctor that I always dreamed about. Thank you so much for everything that you did for me, Uncle Frankie. I love you." She kissed the picture and placed it back in its place in on the nightstand.

The first night on her own, she had a nightmare about Uncle Frankie. His voice was as clear in her dream as it was the last time she heard his voice when he was living.

I am here to protect you, and as long as I am alive, I'm all the protection that you will ever need. Frankie said in her dream.

What about when you're no longer alive? Who will protect me then? Avery asked. His lips were moving, but she couldn't hear what he was saying. His face contorted in pain and then he faded away. She screamed and reached for Frankie, but he was gone.

Avery woke up panting and in a sweat. Santos whined a little and then hopped in bed with her to settle her.

"Another bad dream, boy. I'm sorry I woke you up." She rubbed his head and laid back down in the bed.

While most college students were out enjoying the college party life, Avery was focused on completing school and realizing her dreams of becoming a doctor. She decided not to run track, but she did get up every morning and run three miles and train before class. Taking the max load every fall, spring, and summer semester, and completing the requirements for her degree in two years, didn't leave her much time for a social or love life. Avery was accepted into medical school, completing it in another four years, and did her medical residency at the local hospital. At 28, she moved back to Metropolis, Virginia after taking a job at Metropolis Memorial Hospital.

She walked into the back yard and kneeled at the small cross with Santos' name on it. "Hey, old friend. I miss you, boy." She stood and went to the front door and rang the doorbell. Violet opened it.

"I told you that you don't have to ring the doorbell, this is your house, too," Violet said pulling Avery into a big hug.

"I mean, hey, you never know. You might have some strapping young gentleman in here. I don't want to intrude," she said, hugging her back.

"Yeah right," Violet said, pulling away from the hug.

"Aunt Vy, you cut your hair," Avery said, studying her aunt.

"Do you like it, or is it too short? Be honest." Violet ran her hands self-consciously through her short curls.

"Yeah, I like it," Avery answered honestly as she stared at her aunt. She took in all of Violet's features as if she were just seeing her for the first time tonight.

"Well, thanks. Why are you looking at me like that?" Violet asked, walking into the kitchen, and getting them both a bottle of water.

"No reason, you just look amazing." Avery followed her into the kitchen. "So, you know Uncle Frankie has been dead for almost twenty years now, and I think that it is about time you dated someone. There is a neurosurgeon at the hospital that is very handsome, extremely nice, and remarkably successful. His wife passed away two years ago, and he has two adult sons. I was thinking that I can set you guys up on a date." She winked at her aunt and took a drink from her bottle of water.

"Thanks, but no thanks. I'm fine by myself," Violet answered as she took a drink from her bottle.

"Will you do it for me? Please?" Avery gave her aunt the puppy dog eyes that she used to use on Uncle Frankie all those years ago.

Violet laughed. "Ok. But under one condition."

"What?" Avery asked.

"You have to be there and bring a date, too," Violet countered as she took another drink from the bottle.

"Um, how, and who?" Avery asked.

"I don't know, but I guess you better get to looking." Violet stood and walked out of the kitchen.

Avery laughed, collected both bottles of water and followed her aunt into the living room. "Well, I better run. My shift starts in an hour. I just wanted to visit you and Santos for a minute. You know that there is always an open invitation to my house, Aunt Vy." She hugged her aunt tight.

"I know, baby. I will. I'm giving you time to get settled. Besides, I wouldn't want to walk in on something." Violet wiggled her eyebrows at Avery.

"You definitely don't have to worry about that. Love you, Aunt Vy." Avery opened the front door and turned back to her aunt. "Still having dinner tomorrow night?"

"Sure are. Those dinners are the highlight of my week. And I love you, too." Violet hugged her again.

Avery started for the hospital, finishing her bottle of water on the way, and sitting Violet's bottle of water in her cup holder. When she made it to the hospital she went to her office, taking and labeling the samples and then delivering them to the lab. The ER was quiet that afternoon and evening. A little boy came in with a broken arm after falling off his bike, an elderly lady came in with the flu, and the other patients she saw were non-emergency issues that could have been handled by a primary physician the following morning. On her lunch break, she made her way to Dr. Williams' office and knocked on the door.

"Come in," he answered. "Hi, Avery. How are you?" he smiled.

"I'm very well, thank you, Harrison." Avery answered as she took the seat on the other side of his desk. "So, I told you about my gorgeous, single, aunt the other day. I was wondering if you would be interested in having dinner with us tomorrow night."

"Oh, really? Well, I mean I guess so. You know that I haven't dated anyone since Janet passed away, and we were married for thirty-eight years." He sighed. "Does she really want to go out with me?"

Avery held back her laughter as she saw this brilliant doctor who saved countless lives every day, be as nervous as a pig in a bacon factory at the idea of going out with her aunt. "Yes, she does, but I need to ask a favor of you."

"Ok." Harrison said.

"I have to bring a date as well, so I was wondering if you can possibly bring Mikel with you." Avery winced as she finished her sentence.

"My son, Mikel?" Harrison asked.

"Yeah. I don't know of anyone else, and from what you say, he is single, so I thought that you could bring him. He doesn't have to be my date, just a companion for the evening. That is the one condition that my aunt gave," Avery said.

"Ok." Harrison gave Avery a huge smile.

"Just like that? You think he will come?" She asked.

"Of course, he will. He loves spending time with his old man." Harrison gave her a wink.

"Great. Thanks, Harrison. Dinner is at seven at Downtown Moretti's. You guys like Italian?" she asked as she walked towards the office door.

"Our favorite," Harrison said.

"Fantastic! See you guys tomorrow." Avery exited his office and then answered her ringing phone.

"Av, come upstairs and meet your niece," Tonya said on the other end.

"What? You had her already. Why didn't you call me sooner? What room number?" Avery asked as she headed towards the elevator. She exited the elevator and knocked on the hospital room door.

"Come in," Tonya called back.

Avery entered the room with a huge smile on her face. "Oh, my goodness. Let me meet my niece." She went straight for the baby and took her out of Tonya's arms.

"Hey to you, too," Tonya said.

"I'm sorry, chica. How are you, Mommy? Do you feel ok? Have they been in to check on you?" Avery morphed into doctor mode.

"I'm fine, I'm fine. We're fine." Tonya smiled adorningly at her baby girl and then at Tony behind her.

"Tony, you did a good job." Avery said as she smiled lovingly at the miracle in her arms.

"No, we did a good job." He stood and kissed his wife on her lips.

"Who would have thought that we would be here?" Tonya said to Tony.

"I did. You guys have been hot and heavy since the tenth grade. True love. And now we have this perfect angel from your love." Avery said. She was already in love with the little one.

"Yeah, he is pretty great, that's why I married him." Tonya angled her head up for another kiss.

"We want to ask you to be the Godmother," Tony said.

"It would be an honor. I need to take a picture and send to Brad. I'm sure he will be by to see you guys. Well, he and Katie will be by," Avery added.

"Are you jealous that Brad is getting some and you aren't?" Tonya laughed.

"No, I am not jealous. I am happy for him. In fact, they are getting married next month," Avery answered.

"That's great. Alicia and her flavor of the month should be here soon. If you want to stay," Tonya said.

"I will have to catch her at your house when you go home, my lunch is almost over." Avery touched the baby girl's cheek. "Did you guys come up with a name yet?" she asked.

Tony and Tonya looked at each other and Tonya answered. "Well, we wanted to name her after you."

"Me?" Avery asked.

"Yeah, you. You have always been there for us, especially when Tony lost his job, and we almost lost our home. We can never repay you for everything that you have done for us. We love you so much," Tonya said.

"I love you guys, too." Avery smiled at her friend. "You don't want to name her Avery or Elaine, so how about we name her Alexandria?" Avery suggested.

"I like that. Alexandria Marie Coleman. That's perfect." Tony said.

"I like it too, baby. So, we will name her Alexandria Marie Coleman." Tonya said.

Avery smiled at baby Alexandria and handed her back to her mother. "Tony, brush up on your Spanish. My baby is going to be bilingual, Spanish being her first language." Avery teased.

"Hey, my Spanish might not be perfect, but I can manage." Tony laughed. "A brother is just trying to make it. Tonya speaks enough Spanish for both of us. Especially when she is mad and cussing me out."

"Watch it." Tonya teased.

"You know I love you. I mean, te amo." Tony said, causing Avery and Tonya to laugh.

"Ok. I will be back to check on you later. Call me if you need me. Love you guys." Avery hugged them both and headed back down to the ER to finish her shift.

"How do I look?" Violet asked as she made a circle in her form fitting black dress with black opened toe heels.

"You look beautiful. You always look beautiful. And that booty looks amazing. Have you upped your squats lately?" Avery asked Violet.

"Yeah, and I have added yoga to my daily workout. You don't think this is too tight. I mean, I am fifty now." Violet smoothed her hands down her black dress.

"Aunt Vy, you have the body of a thirty-year-old, you might as well show it off. It's not like you're dressed like a street walker. You look very nice. And hot. And sexy." Avery winked at her. "He is gonna love it."

"You look amazing as well. Do you know how long it has been since I have seen you in anything other than that white coat and scrubs?" Violet asked as she grabbed her purse.

"Do you know how long it has been since I have worn anything other than that white coat and scrubs? Besides my running clothes, I never get a chance to dress up." Avery suddenly felt a little self-conscious in her sleeveless navy bandage dress paired with her black stiletto heels.

"That Mikel is a lucky fellow." Violet grabbed Avery's hand as they left the house to go on their double date.

"Hey Pops. Sorry I'm late. I had to run home and shower." Mikel hugged his father.

"No, problem, son. I'm glad you changed before you came." Harrison sighed.

"Oh, no. What is it, Pops?" Mikel asked suspiciously.

"I want you to meet someone." Harrison said.

"Pops, really? After you tried to set me up with Susie or Mary, or whatever her name was, and she turned out to be completely psycho, I thought that you would have learned your lesson." Mikel laughed.

"She seemed like a nice young lady at church. And her name was Karen. You shouldn't have had sex with her." Harrison scolded his son as they walked into the restaurant.

"Pops, I'm a thirty-four-year-old, healthy, virile, and handsome black man. What did you expect to happen? She was fine. Maybe I should give her a call." Mikel joked.

Harrison gave his son a look and Mikel laughed. "I'm just joking, Pops. Who is it this time?" Mikel asked.

"It's a nice young lady who works at the hospital with me." Harrison said.

"A nurse?" Mikel questioned his father.

"No, a doctor, and it's a double date. Her aunt wouldn't go out with me unless she brought a date, so I'm bringing you. Try to act like your mother and I raised you right." Harrison said.

"Look at you. Pops trying to get some pus-" Mikel stopped himself before his father smacked him. "I'm sorry, Pops. I got you." Mikel said.

"Ok, Aunt Violet, that's him there in the navy blazer." Avery pointed out Harrison for her aunt.

"Damn, he is fine. How old did you say he was?" Violet asked as they stood to greet their suitors.

"He is fifty-eight." Avery said under her breath as she went to greet Harrison.

"Hello, Harrison." Avery hugged him. "This is my aunt, Violet Jones. Aunt Violet, this is Dr. Harrison Williams." Avery stepped aside as they shook each other hands. She smiled as Harrison complimented Violet and she blushed and giggled. They started a conversation and completely forgot about Avery and Mikel."

"Hey, I'm Mikel." Mikel offered his hand.

"Oh, I'm sorry." Avery turned to Mikel. "I'm…" She laid her eyes upon the most perfect specimen of a man she had ever seen. He stood around 6'2", had sparkling brown eyes, and perfect teeth. His skin was the color of milk chocolate, and he had a perfect haircut and perfectly trimmed goatee. His fingernails were cut low, and they were clean. Avery always admired a well-groomed man. She glanced at his white button up shirt, khaki pants, and brown loafers. She cleared her throat to gather her wits and then offered her hand. "I'm Avery Jones. Nice to meet you, Mikel Williams." She said.

He offered her a smile. "Or just Mikel. You don't have to be so formal."

"Ok. Mikel." Avery laughed nervously.

"Jones, party of four." The hostess called out.

"That's us, you guys." Avery said.

They followed the hostess to their seats. Harrison pulled out Violet's chair for her and then placed it under her as she sat. She thanked him, and he took the seat next to her. Avery waited for Mikel to pull out her chair, but instead he took the seat in front of his father. Avery took a seat in the empty chair. Harrison gave Mikel a look that could kill. Mikel, realizing his mistake apologized to Avery.

"That's fine." She said as she opened her menu.

Mikel opened his menu but couldn't concentrate on it. He tried to resist glancing at Avery, but he couldn't help it. She was stunning, and so was her aunt. She had a short, pixie haircut that showcased her beautiful curly hair. She was about 5'7" with a perfect natural body. She had average sized, perky breasts and legs that went on for days and finally met a perfectly round butt. It wasn't too big, and it wasn't too small, it was just right. She was in great shape, and it showed. Her skin was a perfect chestnut brown, and she had a small hump in her nose that fit her face perfectly. He tried not to stare at the perfect pair of lips that she covered in a plum-colored lipstick, and her perfume had his senses on edge. He thought for a minute that he forgot how to read as he just stared at the menu.

Avery peered over her menu at her aunt. She was smiling and laughing with Harrison. Avery then glanced at Harrison and saw that he had a twinkle in his eye as he laughed and talked with Violet.

Avery watched the exchange and smiled. She looked over at Mikel and found him staring at her.

"Are you ok? Your pupils look a little dilated." Avery asked as she stared at him.

"Um, yeah. I'm ok." Mikel turned his attention back to the menu in his hand.

Harrison looked at Mikel and let out a chuckle. "He is fine, Avery." Harrison looked at his son and winked. Mikel shifted in his seat a little. Harrison knew why his pupils were dilated; he was very interested in little Miss Avery.

The waitress came to their table and took their orders. When their drinks arrived, Avery savored her wine. "Umm. This is so good." She all but moaned.

Mikel stared at Avery as his manhood jumped a little at her moans. He shifted in his seat and took a big gulp of his beer.

"Avery, where have you been hiding this extraordinary woman?" Harrison asked.

"I've only been working at the hospital for six months now." Avery laughed. "If I knew that you guys would hit it off so well, I would have introduced you to each other sooner." She winked at Aunt Violet.

"Oh, Harrison. Stop it." Violet blushed and playfully hit Harrison with her cloth napkin.

Avery leaned over and whispered to Mikel, "I think that we hit a homerun with these two."

"Yeah, I think we did." Mikel said while looking at Avery.

As the four of them made small talk, the waitress brought their food to the table. As they ate, Harrison and Violet were in their own little world, leaving Avery and Mikel no choice but to make conversation with each other.

"So, Mikel, what do you do for a living?" Avery asked.

"I'm a homicide detective for Metropolis Police Department." He answered.

"Oh, so you, too are no stranger to death." She replied.

"Unfortunately, no, I'm not." Mikel said. "How old are you?"

"Twenty-eight. You?" She countered.

"Thirty-four." He ate a forkful of his pasta before speaking again. "Do you have any kids?"

"Oh, no. No, no, no, no, no." She said. They both laughed.

"Why did you say it like that?" Mikel said.

"I'm just saying. No, I don't have any kids. I've never been married, I don't have some psycho ex, nor do I have a current boyfriend. You?" Avery said.

"I have five kids, four baby mommas, an ex-wife, and a dog that is mean as hell." He said.

Avery choked on her pasta. She took a swallow of water before she responded. "Oh, ok. Well, you are a pretty busy man."

"Avery, I'm joking. I don't have any kids or ex-wife. I do have a dog, but she is a sweetheart. Now, I may have a few crazy exes." He admitted with a chuckle.

"Interesting." Avery said.

"What does that mean?" Mikel wanted to know.

"Well, I figure it is one of two things. Either you are attracted to crazy, or you do something to make them crazy." She guessed.

"I plead the fifth." Mikel held up his hands in surrender, making Avery laugh.

Dinner lasted about two and a half hours for the four of them.

"Well, I think that we have held up this table long enough." Harrison said.

"Me, too." Avery echoed.

"Um. Avery, Harrison and I are going to go out for drinks. Maybe Mikel can take you home." Violet said.

Avery went to protest and then stopped. She turned to Mikel. "Do you mind? It's not that far."

"Not at all." Mikel said.

Harrison paid for their dinner, and they said their goodbyes. Avery walked with Mikel to his SUV. He opened the door and helped her inside. He pulled out of the parking lot and drove in the direction of her house.

"So, Ms. Avery Jones, are you single by choice, or have you just not found what you are looking for?" Mikel honesty asked.

"Well, I guess it is a little bit of both. Take this next right." She told him.

"Ok. Career driven, and you don't have time for some knucklehead getting in your way. And I can tell that you aren't too trusting of men, with the exception of my dad." Mikel said.

"Right on all accounts. But how do you know all that?" She asked Mikel.

"I'm in law enforcement, I pick up on things like that. Your body language suggests that you are ready to mace me at any time." Mikel laughed.

"You would be so lucky to get maced." Avery said jokingly, but seriously. "Since I don't have any mace, you may have to settle for a quick death."

"Oh, it's like that. Ok. I hear you." Mikel laughed.

Avery laughed, too, because he didn't know that she wasn't joking. They pulled to her driveway, and he stopped at the gate. Avery punched the code in her phone and the gate opened.

"Nice place." Mikel said as her house came into view. He could see the moon glistening off the lake in the distance behind the house.

"Thanks." Avery pushed a series of codes on her phone as they made their way to the front door. She opened the front door and invited him in. "I don't think that I have any beer in the fridge, but I do have some wine."

"Ok." Mikel smiled as he entered her home. She locked the door behind him, and he followed her into the kitchen.

"Red or white?" She asked as she held up two bottles of wine.

"Surprise me." He said.

"Ok, white it is." Avery got two wine glasses from the cabinet and filled them both. She motioned for Mikel to follow her into the living room where she turned on the TV and handed him a glass of wine. "I'll be right back." She went into her bedroom and changed from her heels to a pair of flip flops then joined Mikel on the sofa.

"So, Mikel, how long have you been a detective?" She asked, taking a sip of wine.

"Eight years. But I've been on the force since I was 21. Started out patrolling the streets." Mikel answered.

"You didn't want to be a doctor like your dad?" Avery asked.

"No, I didn't. I tried it, but deep down I always wanted to be a police officer. However, my big brother always wanted to be a doctor like my dad. He is a pediatrician, I'm sure you already know that." Mikel said.

"Yes, I know. I see him when he comes to visit your dad. I have never seen you other than on pictures." Avery finished her glass of wine and went into the kitchen to get the bottle. She brought it back to the living room and refilled both of their glasses.

"So, Ms. Avery Jones," Mikel started.

"Just Avery." She giggled.

"You got me. So, Avery, what's the best part of your job?"

"Saving lives." She answered honestly. "And the worst part is losing them."

"I know what you mean. I have seen it all. It seems that gang violence is the worst and hardest to solve. We are even getting gang activity around here from California. It's crazy." Mikel took another drink of his wine.

"Really? Wow." Avery commented as she finished her second glass of wine. She poured the rest of the bottle in her glass.

"Yeah. It's something else. Ok. Enough about work. What do you do in your spare time?" Mikel reached out and put his hand on her knee. She moved his hand and put it back in his lap.

"I read, and I like to run. I actually love to run." She said.

"Read and run. Anything else?" Mikel asked.

"Well, yeah. Read, run, and work." Avery finished her glass of wine and sat it on the table.

"Sounds pretty boring." Mikel laughed. "Did you spike this wine with something? I feel a little buzzed."

Avery laughed at Mikel. "You are a light weight. No, I didn't put anything in your wine. It definitely gives you a buzz and is a little on the strong side, but I can't believe that you are drunk."

"Not drunk, buzzed." Mikel unbuttoned his shirt and took it off, revealing his muscular physique in the white t-shirt that he now wore. Avery discreetly inhaled his scent. He smelled like a mixture of expensive cologne and all man. The scent was intoxicating and made goosebumps form on her skin.

"What do you do for fun, Mikel?" Avery asked sarcastically.

"Shoot pool. Shoot basketball. Swim. Take Raven to the park."
Mikel answered.

"Interesting. What kind of dog do you have?"

"I have no idea; she is a mutt. I found her under my car one day
when she was a puppy, and I have had her ever since." Mikel said.

"That's sweet." Avery collected the wine glasses and placed them
in the kitchen sink.

Mikel yawned. "I better get going, Avery."

"Oh, no. You can pick any of the guest rooms to sleep in. You
aren't driving anywhere buzzed, lightweight." She laughed as she
grabbed his hand and led him to the first guest bedroom and turned
on the light. She pointed to the opened door inside the room. "There's
your bathroom. It has towels and toiletries in there if you need them.
Good night." She shut the door behind her and went through the
house turning off the lights and TV. She set the alarm and went
to her bedroom, locking the door behind her. After showering and
climbing into the bed, she saw that it was 1:30 in the morning. It
wasn't long before she was sound asleep. Avery was awakened by the
light beeping of her alarm by her bed. She looked at her phone and
saw that it was the front door. Reaching under her pillow, she grabbed
her gun and lightly and swiftly walked to the front door. She went
through the kitchen and saw a silhouette in the dark at her front door.
She walked up behind them and put the gun to the figure's head.

He instantly knew that the cold metal he felt against the back of
his head was a gun. "What the fuck, Avery? It's me, Mikel." He held
up his hands.

Avery turned on the light and disarmed her alarm using her fin-
gerprint. "What the fuck to you! I almost killed you!" Avery yelled
back at him.

"Damn, you weren't going to give a warning? Why in the hell do you have a gun and how did you sneak up on me like that?" Mikel asked.

"What in the hell are you doing? You should have let me know that you were leaving, and I would have disarmed the alarm." Avery let out an angry deep breath to calm herself. She looked at Mikel. "You should have let me know you were leaving." She spoke a lot calmer this time.

"I'm sorry. I was just going to leave and go home. I didn't want to wake you. I didn't know that you would go all Rambo on my ass. Shit!"

"You've seen *Rambo?*" Avery asked, amused.

Mikel smiled. "I don't know how you find humor in this. You almost killed me." He laughed a little.

"Yeah, sorry about that." Avery said. "My alarm went off and I thought someone was breaking in."

"I didn't hear your alarm." It dawned on him that she had a silent alarm that went off first. "Silent alarm. Ok." Mikel looked at Avery for the first time noticing that she only had on a camisole and underwear. Her nipples were peeking through the silky material.

Avery looked down at herself and saw what had caught Mikel's attention. "Ok. Time to go." She unlocked the double locks on the door and opened it for Mikel.

"Thanks for letting me crash at your place." Mikel stood so close to her that she could smell his musk.

"You're welcome." She whispered, her throat suddenly becoming dry.

"Can I have your number?" He reached out and touched her shoulder and started his decent to her breasts. She grabbed his hand and stopped him.

"Hand me your phone." She said.

He unlocked his phone and handed it to her. She put her number in his phone and put space between herself and Mikel. "I'll see you later. Be careful going home." Avery said.

Mikel laughed and told her that he would call her later. On the drive home, he thought to himself that he had lost his touch. Usually women fell at his feet, but Avery Jones was no ordinary woman. The more he thought about her, the more he realized that he wanted to know more about her. "Avery Jones." He said to himself and smiled as he pulled into his driveway.

CHAPTER 10

"Hello." Avery said.

"Hey, Avery Jones. It's Mikel."

"Good morning, Mikel. To what do I owe this pleasure?" Avery poured herself a cup of coffee.

"I was just wondering if you were free tonight. Around seven." Mikel asked.

"Maybe. Why?" She asked.

"Dinner, tonight. That is if you think that you can go one night without trying to kill me." Mikel laughed into the phone.

Avery smiled. "Well, I may be able to go one night without trying to kill you. At least I will try. But it needs to be more around eight."

"As long as these fools don't kill anyone on the streets between now and then, I will be there." Mikel suddenly felt nervous.

"Ok. Well, I have to go. I will see you around eight. Buzz me when you get to the gate." She said her goodbyes and ended the call. She didn't know why she said yes to Mikel Williams, but she was kind of glad that she did.

"Yes, Aunt Vy, we are going to dinner." Avery put on a pair of gold hoop earrings while talking to her aunt on the phone.

"I'm just in shock, is all. I mean you have probably only been on five dates your whole life." Violet said as she pushed the button to open her gate.

"That's four more than I have seen you go on in the last eighteen years." Avery laughed.

"Touché, little one, touché." Violet said.

Avery heard the doorbell through the phone. "Who is ringing your doorbell at 7:55 at night?" Avery asked Violet.

"Harrison. And make that three. I will talk to you later. Love you." Violet hung up the phone and Avery laughed as she sprayed on her perfume. "It's about damn time, Aunt Vy." She said aloud before she heard the buzzer from the front gate.

She pushed the intercom. "Yes, may I help you?"

"It's me, Mikel." He said smoothly into the intercom.

"Mikel who?" Avery said.

"Mikel Williams. I told you I would be here at eight." He said.

"Um, I'm sorry. That name doesn't ring a bell. Have a good night." Avery turned off the intercom and watched Mikel's face on the screen from the camera at the gate. He sat there with his mouth hanging opened.

"Close your mouth, Mikel. It was a joke." She opened the gate. She saw Mikel smile as he pulled through the gate and to the house. Reaching the front door, he rang the doorbell.

Avery opened the door and smiled. Mikel stepped in and pulled her close to him with one hand, surprising her, and forcing her not to break his arm on reflex.

"So, you have jokes, huh?" He said, looking lustily into her eyes. He looked her up and down, taking in her ankle cropped jeans, white shirt, her striped blazer, and ankle booties. She politely squeezed out of his embrace and smiled.

"Yeah, sometimes I do. Let me grab my wallet and I will be ready to go." She said.

On the ride to the restaurant, they made small talk before Avery asked him about his dad and Violet.

"Did you know that your dad and my aunt have another date tonight?" She asked.

"Yeah, I do, and I'm happy for him. He hasn't smiled this much or been this excited since before my mom died. And he looks at your aunt like he looked at my mom. It may be love at first sight for them." Mikel said.

"You think?" She questioned.

"I don't know, maybe. Especially if she gives him some. Pops would lose his mind." Mikel laughed.

"Please don't spoil my appetite, Mikel. I seriously doubt that will happen. My aunt hasn't had a man in the eighteen years we have been together, and I highly doubt she will give it up to your father. She has only known him, what, a week?" Avery said.

Mikel let out a loud chuckle. "All the more reason why it will probably happen. My dad hasn't had sex since before my mom died. She was sick for the last year of her life before she passed away. Do you really think that two people who feel a connection with each other as much as they do, and who haven't been physical with another human being in years won't make something happen? Hell, it wouldn't surprise me if they skipped dinner and got it on and popping instead." He laughed again, but Avery didn't.

She picked up her phone and texted her aunt. *Don't do anything that I wouldn't do.*

She waited for a response. *Too late.* 😊

"What in the hell?" Avery stared at her phone.

Just kidding. Relax. You just enjoy that piece of eye candy that you are going out with tonight. Me and Harrison are just fine.

Avery smiled before she texted back. *Ok. Goodnight.*

Goodnight.

Violet placed her phone on the nightstand and looked at Harrison's naked body.

"I almost forgot what it was like." She smiled.

Harrison drew circles with his fingers on her hip as he gazed into her eyes. "Seems like you remembered pretty well to me." They both laughed as he pulled her close to him for a kiss. His manhood jumped and made her laugh.

"I think he wants some more." Harrison started kissing down her neck and then down farther and farther.

"Umm. He can have it." Violet moaned as she rubbed the back of Harrison's head.

Mikel took Avery to a seafood restaurant on the river.

"I've never been here, Mikel. It's so nice." Avery took the seat offered to her by Mikel.

"Me, either." Mikel laughed. "Full disclosure, I'm just trying to impress you, Doc."

"Well, score one for you." Avery smiled before she frowned. "Not really score, you aren't scoring with me or anything." She shook her head. "Is it hot in here?" Avery started to fan herself with her menu. She had succeeded in embarrassing herself.

Mikel sat in his chair, crossing his arms and smiling at her.

"You know what I meant." Avery said.

"Hey, I didn't say anything." Mikel said, picking up his menu. "So, what are you thinking about having?" He asked, peering over his menu and winking at her.

"Definitely not that." Avery said, flipping the page on her menu, causing Mikel to laugh. "I was thinking maybe of going with the grilled shrimp salad."

"Salad? Girl, what? You better get something to fill you up." Mikel looked over his menu one last time. "I think I am going to get the surf and turf."

"That sounds delicious. I think I will get the cheesy lobster dip for an appetizer." Avery placed her menu down on the table.

"Sounds pretty good." Mikel placed his menu on the table and took a drink of water. "I have been thinking about you for the past week."

"Really? What did you come up with?" Avery asked.

"Well, from our conversations, I think that you are a pretty ba-dass doctor. Compassionate. Beautiful. Unbelievably sexy. Funny. Intelligent. And you don't take any shit. I think I like it." Mikel drank some more water.

"Oh, I thought that you were going to tell me something that I didn't already know." Avery took a drink from her wine glass.

Mikel laughed, which made Avery smile. "You're not like the women I usually date." He admitted. The waitress took their orders before Avery responded.

"Yeah, how so? Not crazy enough? And who said we are dating?" She asked.

"Well, you're just the right amount of crazy, and we are on a date, aren't we?" He asked. "And I can't really explain it. I don't know how to put it into words, it's more of a feeling." Mikel shrugged. "It's actually kind of scary."

"I think you should be scared." Avery retorted.

"Oh, it's like that, huh?" Mikel said.

Avery's lobster dip arrived at the table, and she dipped her chip into it and tasted it. Mikel reached on the plate for a chip and Avery smacked his hand away.

"I'm sorry, you ordered what you wanted. This is all mine." Avery made a show of eating the dip and commenting on how good it was.

"Really?" Mikel asked.

Avery rolled her eyes. "Here, Tramp." She slid the plate into the middle of the table.

Mikel couldn't help but be amused at her *Lady and the Tramp* reference. Over cheesy lobster dip and dinner, they learned more about each other. Avery was quite smitten with the detective, sometimes bad boy, that was a sensitive and caring guy at heart. Mikel was absolutely head over heels for Avery, the woman that kept him on his toes and that was working her way into his heart without even trying to or knowing that she was.

"I have been meaning to ask you what's in your locket." He pointed to her necklace.

Instinctively, Avery reached for the necklace and held it in her hand. She took a deep breath and opened it. "It's my Uncle Frankie. He passed away eighteen years ago." Avery could feel her eyes starting to water. After all this time, she still hurt and longed for her uncle.

Mikel noticed the change in her demeanor and apologized. "Hey, Av, I'm sorry." He reached over the table to grab her hand. She let him hold her hand for a second before placing it in her lap.

"It's fine. He was just very important to me, and when he died all those years ago, a piece of me died as well." She closed the locket. "I have had this since I was ten, and I never take it off." She cleared her throat.

Against his better judgement, he decided to ask what has been on his mind since the first night he met her. "Why don't you trust men?"

"People. I don't trust people in general." She answered.

"Yeah, but you especially don't trust men, except for my dad. For every inch that you open up to me, you take two inches back." Mikel said.

"What do you want me to say? You want me to say that my father used to beat my mother, and that she died in a car accident when I was a baby, so I have no memory of her. Let's see what else? My Uncle Frankie raised me from a baby until he died when I was ten. He was the best part of my life. He loved me more than anyone else in this world could ever have loved me." Avery couldn't stop the tears from flowing. She had not spoken of her Uncle Frankie in years, and it still hurt her to think about him. "Do you want me to say that my father killed my uncle in front of me? Is that what you want to hear? Do you want to hear that I have never let a man close to me because I don't know who I can trust, I don't know when someone will turn out to be the bad guy? How about me telling you that I trust your dad because he reminds me of my Uncle Frankie? He loves his family and would do anything to protect them. He is honest and stands for what he believes in no matter what. Is that what you want me to say? Huh? Is that what you want to hear?" Avery slammed her napkin on the table and stormed off to the bathroom. She felt like a fool. She hadn't shed many tears in the last eighteen years, and she didn't plan on shedding any now. She was thankful that the bathroom was empty as she went into the first stall and cried. She wanted to sit down, but she most certainly was not going to sit on a public toilet. She heard the door open and tried to calm herself before the woman entering the restroom thought that she was crazy. She saw a hand reach over the top of the stall and offer her a cloth napkin. Avery noticed that the hand belonged to Mikel.

"I'm sorry, Avery. I didn't mean to upset you. I'm a dumbass at times." Mikel said.

Avery let out a small laugh. "No, you're not. I shouldn't have blown up like that. Well, maybe you are just a little." She laughed again.

"Will you please come out? I already paid the bill and I have your wallet. We can go. Plus, I kind of shouldn't be in the women's bathroom." Mikel said.

Avery laughed and opened the door. "No, you shouldn't be. We can go."

She started for the door, but Mikel caught her arm and pulled her into a hug. She was tense at first, then she relaxed, and wrapped her arms around him. She had never hugged a man intimately, other than her Uncle Frankie.

"You ready?" He asked. She nodded, and he grabbed her hand, leading her out of the bathroom, and then out of the restaurant.

"I'm sorry, Mikel. I usually never lose it like that." Avery explained once they were in the car.

"I know, but you needed to. That's a lot to carry around." He reasoned. He continued driving the route to her house. "You know, I was a momma's boy from the time I was born. I remember when my dad told my brother and me that our mother was sick. I could see in his eyes that it wasn't good. She had ovarian cancer. She lived for two years after her diagnosis, and I saw everyday how much my dad loved and cared for her, and how everyday it killed him that he couldn't save her." Mikel let out a deep breath. "I know how losing someone so important to you feels, and I can only imagine how much it has affected you and your aunt."

"Yeah." Was all Avery said.

"When my mother died, I felt like my world came to an end. She was always there for me, keeping me straight, teaching me how to love, and loving me unconditionally. I miss hearing her sweet voice on the phone when she would call fussing at me for not calling her all day. I miss hugging her. I miss the smell of her. I miss her Sunday dinners. I miss everything about her, but it gets a little easier every day." They drove in silence for the remainder of the ride to Avery's house.

Once they made it to the house, Avery apologized again.

"I'm sorry I ruined our date."

"Are you kidding me? You didn't ruin anything." He reached out to caress her cheek and smiled. "You just said it was a date." He continued to smile.

Avery smiled back. "Do you want a drink on the lake? It's beautiful this time of night."

"Sure." He followed her inside.

She grabbed the wine, glasses, a flashlight, and then he followed her to the back door. Avery unlocked the back gate, and they walked down to the pier holding hands. She unlocked the boathouse and grabbed a blanket and pillows. Mikel joined her on the wicker sofa and looked out over the lake.

"This is amazing, Avery." Mikel held her in his arms.

"Yeah, it is. It's like heaven on earth." She replied.

They sat there in each other's arms watching the moonlight dance across the water.

"Are you hiding from your dad?" Mikel asked.

Avery tensed up before she relaxed. "What makes you think that I'm hiding from someone?" She asked.

"It's my job to notice things, Avery. You have your house secured better than Alcatraz."

Avery laughed.

"Whereas most people would have their homes closer to the water and have a fence that doesn't obstruct this magnificent view, you have your house farther away from the water and your fence completely blocks any view you have of the water. Your best view is when you pull in through the gate." Mikel let his hands glide up and down her arms.

"I'm not hiding from anyone, just being careful." Avery admitted.

"Ok." Was Mikel's only reply.

They sat at the water talking for another hour over wine before they went back into the house. "I better go, it's getting late."

"You can stay if you want. You know, in the guest room." Avery said.

"Cool, but first, I'm going to kiss you." Mikel noticed that Avery looked terrified at the thought of him kissing her. "Or not." He said.

She shook her head. "No, it's not you, it's me."

"It's fine, Avery. I can wait." Mikel surprised himself with that statement. Usually, he has slept with the woman of the moment by the second date, but Avery wasn't like those women. She was strong and tough, but fragile and insecure at the same time. He knew that she didn't tell him the entire truth, and she was hiding from something or someone, but he had to admit that she didn't seem scared. She seemed cautious, but not scared.

He took the guest room that he slept in the first night, only he didn't get any sleep. By midnight, he heard a soft knock on his door.

"Mikel, are you asleep?" Avery whispered.

"No, I'm not," he replied.

"Can I come in?" She asked.

"Yep." Mikel sat up in the bed.

"I can't sleep," she whispered, sitting on the edge of the bed.

"Me either," Mikel admitted.

"I have to tell you something." Avery turned to face Mikel, taking in his muscular physique in the bed.

"Ok." Mikel responded cautiously.

"I've never been kissed." She blurted out.

"Like ever?" Mikel asked.

"Ever. I've only been on three dates, and they were in college and med school." Avery admitted.

Mikel scooted closer to her. "Do you want me to kiss you?" He asked in a husky voice.

Avery nodded her head, yes.

Mikel leaned in, and lifting her chin with his finger, gently pushed his lips to hers. Her lips were so warm and soft. He felt a surge of energy shoot through his body. He pulled away and looked at Avery, knowing she felt it, too.

She smiled. "That was nice. Do it again."

He kissed her again, and she eagerly kissed him back, timidly easing her tongue into his mouth. He nibbled and then sucked her tongue, before entangling his tongue with hers. She deepened the kiss, and he stopped her.

"As much as I want to, we can't. I'm a lot more experienced than you, and you don't want to do something that you can't take back." Mikel noticed that her nipples poked through her top, and he cursed under his breath.

"You're right. I better go." Avery exited his room and entered hers.

"You are a damn fool, Mikel." He said to himself. He went down the hallway and walked to what he assumed was her bedroom door and got ready to knock. He heard buzzing on the other side of the door and laughed to himself before heading back to the guest room to try to sleep.

Mikel and Raven waited at the park for Avery. He saw her pull her black Merecedes SUV into a parking spot and watched as she strolled towards them. She was so beautiful to him.

"Hey, you." Mikel hugged her.

"Hey. This must be Raven." Avery offered her hand to Raven and let her smell. Raven then licked her hand. Avery bent down to rub the black and white mixed breed dog. Raven laid on her back and waited for Avery to rub her belly. Mikel smiled as he watched to two play.

"I figured we could go for a run with Raven," he said.

"That would be fun." Avery rubbed Raven one more time. Being with Raven made her really miss Santos.

They started stretching, preparing to run.

"So, I was thinking we could run the trail that leads back to the track. It's about two miles. Are you ok with that?" Mikel asked

Avery laughed. "Yeah, I'm ok with that."

They both put in their earbuds, and Mikel removed Avery's left earbud and listened.

"Eminem. Ok. I like it." He placed it back in her ear.

Avery took a listen to Mikel's music. "*Eye of The Tiger*. Ok, Rocky, let's go." Avery started jogging, and Raven took off behind her, pulling Mikel along.

By the mile and a half mark, Mikel was tired, but he wouldn't let Avery know. She looked over at Mikel and saw that he looked like he was about to pass out, so she slowed her pace to a brisk walk. Mikel did the same.

"You ok?" Avery asked.

"Yeah, I'm good." Mikel answered while trying to catch his breath.

"Trying to impress me again?" She winked.

"Yeah, is it working?" He bent over, putting his hands on his knees.

"Well, you get an A for effort. Why didn't you say that you weren't a runner?" Avery squatted down beside him.

"I was trying to do something that you liked, and figured I could just, you know, wing it." Mikel said.

"A word of advice, instead of just lifting weights in the gym, add in some cardio. It will increase your stamina." Avery patted him on the back before standing and grabbing the leash for Raven to join her on the last leg of the run.

"I have plenty of stamina." Mikel yelled after Avery. He started off behind them, trying to catch up.

The next morning, Mikel got out of bed and was stiff as a board. Raven jumped around Mikel as he hobbled to the bathroom.

"Damn, what was I thinking." He ran the tub with water as hot as he could stand, added Epsom salts, and got in. "Add more cardio, huh. She thinks I'm punk." Mikel said as he eased his body into the tub.

CHAPTER 11

IIIIIIIIIIIIIIIIIIIIIIIIIIIIIIIIIIIIIIIIIIIIIIIIIIIIIIIIIIIIIIIIIIIIIIIIIIIIIIIIII

"So, what do you want to do tonight?" Mikel asked into the phone while he completed his paperwork.

Avery turned off the lights in her office and shut the door. "I don't know. What did you have in mind?" She asked.

"Well, you could pack a bag and spend the night. I could cook one of my famous dishes and then we could watch a movie. Keep it simple." Mikel suggested.

"Um." Avery hesitated.

"No, Avery, not like that. Unless you want to. You know I'm down." Mikel said.

Avery laughed. "Yeah, I know that you are. If you don't try anything, I'll stay. You do stay at my house quite a bit."

"Yes, I do. I promise to be a complete gentleman. I just want to spend time with you. No funny business." He promised.

"Ok. I will go home and pack a bag. I'm about to head to the parking lot and my phone will lose reception, so I will just call you back when I am on my way." She said.

"Ok. Talk to you later." Mikel ended the call and finished his paperwork. He didn't know what it was about Avery that had him so head over heels. He thought that it may be everything about her that drove him crazy and made him think about her every moment that he was away from her. After he completed his paperwork, he made a grocery list for dinner tonight. He made sure to put that strong ass wine that she was always drinking on the list.

Avery arrived at Mikel's and pulled into the garage. She closed the garage and used the spare key to enter the house. The aroma of the meal he was cooking assaulted her nostrils. It smelled amazing.

"My goodness, it smells delicious in here. What are you cooking?" Avery rubbed Raven's head and then hugged Mikel and kissed him on the lips.

"Chicken marsala, homemade mashed potatoes, green beans, rolls, and a salad. And I have a bottle of your favorite wine in the fridge. Help yourself to it." Mikel said.

"How thoughtful of you, Mr. Williams. Let me shower first, and then I will come back for wine." Avery went into the direction of his ensuite bathroom.

Mikel remembered that he bought the soap that she liked and her shampoo and conditioner. He picked up the bag and walked to the bedroom to give it to her. Avery had her back to Mikel while she was undressing in the bedroom. Mikel reached out to tap her on her shoulder. By pure instinct, Avery grabbed his arm and flipped him over her shoulder onto the bedroom floor. By the time he hit the floor, Avery had her knife pressed against his throat. Her eyes widened in surprise as she saw that it was Mikel.

"Shit! I told you never to sneak up on me!" Avery yelled. She saw Raven standing in the doorway looking at the two of them.

Mikel rubbed the back of his head. "Damn, Av, I didn't mean to. I was trying to bring you your favorite soap and the shampoo and conditioner that you use." Mikel pointed to the items that were now strewn across the floor. "Do you insist on killing me? I think I have a concussion." Mikel rubbed his head.

"I'm so sorry, Mikel." Avery kneeled next to him. "Can you see? How many fingers am I holding up? Count backwards from 20. Follow my finger with your eyes. You're ok. Come on, get up." Avery helped Mikel up. "Do you feel dizzy or sick to your stomach?"

"No, I'm fine. I just feel a knot forming on the back of my head." Mikel continued to rub his head.

Avery went into the freezer and got a bag of frozen vegetables and handed them to him. "Put these on the back of your head. I will finish dinner."

Mikel raised his eyebrows at Avery. "I have never even seen you boil water, and now you are telling me that you are going to finish my meal."

"Yep. That's what I am telling you." Avery led him to the couch, handed him the remote and went into the kitchen to finish dinner. She would periodically check on Mikel to see how he was feeling and to make sure that he was ok.

When Avery was done with dinner, she set two plates on the dinner table and called Mikel into the dining room.

"Dinner is served." Avery bowed for dramatics.

Mikel took his place at the table and looked at his plate. "What did you do?"

"Excuse me?" Avery said, placing the two wine glasses on the table.

"Since my mom died, I am the best cook in the family, but I cannot present a plate like this. This is some Martha Stewart type shit. What did you do?" He asked.

"A lady never reveals her secrets." Avery smiled. "Taste it before you are too impressed. I didn't have to do much."

"I mean, I started it, but this looks amazing." Mikel blessed his food and then tasted it. "This is delicious." He continued eating.

Avery blushed a little. "Growing up, we had a chef. I would sneak into the kitchen while he was cooking and ask him to teach me how to cook. I remembered some of what he taught me. And, you have never seen me boil water because you feed me almost every day. Why should I cook?" Avery winked at Mikel.

"Yeah, you're right. Baby, this is so good. Damn. You put your foot in it. These mashed potatoes. And these green beans. Damn, the rolls even taste better." Mikel was eating like he hadn't had a meal in days.

Avery stared at him before she spoke. "Um, are you ok?" She asked.

"Yeah, I am, this is just absolutely amazing. Is there anything that you can't do?" Mikel asked.

Avery shrugged her shoulders. "When I find out, I will let you know."

They both shared a laugh while they continued to enjoy their dinner and talk about how uneventful their day was. As they talked, Avery looked for signs of a concussion, but there weren't any. Mikel was fine, but she still felt bad for almost killing him. Again.

"So, can I expect you to always try to kill me?" Mikel jokingly asked.

"Mikel, I'm sorry. You startled me." Avery said.

"Why are you so jumpy and how in the hell can you do all that you do? Are you sure that it isn't because of your dad?" Mikel narrowed his eyes at her.

"I just haven't felt safe since my Uncle Frankie died. Well, not completely." She admitted as she began clearing the table. Mikel stood to help, but she told him to relax, she could handle it.

"Not even with me?" Mikel asked, caressing her arm.

"I feel comfortable with you, and safer to an extent, but I have almost killed you twice. You need to step it up." She loaded the dishes into the dishwasher.

"Then teach me." Mikel countered.

"Mikel, I'm still in my scrubs and I haven't showered yet. I would rather just take a shower and go to bed." She said.

"Or would you rather I not be able to fully protect you?" Mikel countered again.

Avery thought a moment before speaking. "We will start off slow, me teaching you a few defensive moves. I will teach you what they don't teach you in the police academy." Avery walked into the living room, rearranging the furniture to the corners of the room. Raven sat near the front door watching the two of them.

Avery turned to Mikel. "Ok, come at me."

"What?" He asked.

"Come at me. Try to attack me." She said again.

"Avery, I'm not going to attack you." Mikel crossed his arms in front of his chest.

"Ok, fine. Then I will attack you." Avery charged Mikel, striking him four times, knocking him to the ground before he knew what happened.

"Dammit, Avery. What the fuck are you doing?" Mikel said as he held his side and nose.

"You asked me to teach you. Experience is the best teacher. When I was ten, my uncle's friend almost choked me out." Avery let out a small chuckle and smiled as she reminisced. "I had a bruise around my neck for a week. But guess what. I have never been choked again since that day. Well, not as bad." She shrugged and helped Mikel to his feet.

"Now attack me," she commanded for the second time.

"You are crazy as hell! Do you know that?" Mikel yelled. "You better be glad that I like crazy." He smiled before charging her.

He tried to land two blows, but instead he received four blows from Avery, the last one sending him flying across the room and gasping for air, before falling to the floor again.

She knelt next to him. "You're leaving yourself exposed. I didn't even have to work for that takedown, you gave it to me."

She helped Mikel to his feet once again and showed him his vulnerable spots and how to correct them and better protect himself. After an hour and a half and a busted nose and lip, Mikel decided that he had enough of a lesson for the night.

"You must have been sneaking in cardio during those gym sessions of yours. You could almost keep up." Avery smiled.

"Actually, I have. Working on my stamina." He smirked.

"I bet." She said. "You're a fast learner. Great job." She walked into the bedroom and picked up her bag to shower.

"I'm gonna use my Epsom salt in the bathtub when you finish showering. I'm going to be sore as hell in the morning." Mikel limped to the bathroom to check his face in the mirror.

Avery followed him and watched him check his reflection in the mirror. "You still look good."

"You think I look good, huh?" He cautiously reached out to her and pulled her into his chest.

Avery looked up at him and rubbed his lip with her thumb. "I mean you're alright. Nothing to write home about." She looked from his lips to his eyes and back to his lips. She placed her lips gently against his. "You better put some ice on your lip to draw out some of the swelling."

"Yes, ma'am." Mikel reluctantly released her and exited the bathroom, closing the door behind him.

Avery stared at the back of the closed door. Mikel really tried to do everything to make her comfortable and happy. She took a deep breath. She wondered why she let him so deep into her world, and if she should keep him at arm's length or not. She smiled and held her locket. "You would like him, Uncle Frankie. Even though he is a cop." She said to herself before turning on the shower and getting her washcloth and bath towel from the cabinet. She brought the soap, shampoo, and conditioner into the shower with her. As she showered, she thought of how she and Mikel went toe to toe and how she knocked him on his ass every time. She laughed under the spray of water as she lathered up her hair. "He is so damn crazy, and I think I like it." She said aloud.

Once she finished showering and putting on her pajamas, she opened the bathroom door to find Mikel waiting on her, but at a distance.

"Let me show you something." He grabbed her hand and led her to his dresser. He opened the top drawer and revealed that it was empty. "This is for you. I emptied it so that you can leave some clothes here and you will have them when you come over. I know that I have a whole room at your house, but I want you to be in my room with me." Mikel was nervous because he knew that she could pull away from him at any moment like she has done before.

"Um, ok."

Mikel smiled. "Ok, then."

Avery got into bed while Mikel ran the bathtub full of hot water and Epsom salt. He winced as he lowered his body into the water. He was already feeling the effects of Avery's ass kicking. When he dried off and dressed in his pajama pants, he opened the bathroom door and walked into the bedroom. Avery was under the covers, sound asleep. He eased into the bed next to her and she turned over into his chest. He held her there and placed his cheek to the top of her head. He loved the way she felt in his arms. He inhaled the scent of her freshly washed hair, the fruity shampoo and conditioner tickling his nose. Soon, sleep overtook Mikel as well.

Avery awakened and felt herself lying on something hard. When she looked down, she saw it was Mikel's chest that she was sleeping on. She tried to move, but he held her tight.

"I like you right here," he said.

Avery smiled despite herself. "I have to pee."

He let Avery get up and she went into the bathroom, closing the door behind her. After relieving herself and washing her hands, she studied her reflection in the mirror. She almost didn't notice the woman staring back at her. She looked happy. Content. She tried to keep the smile from forming on her face, but she couldn't. She crawled back into bed and snuggled up against Mikel, accidentally brushing his stiffened manhood.

"Oops. I'm sorry." She said, embarrassment showing on her face.

Mikel laughed. "Hell, I ain't complaining." He said jokingly as she lightly punched him in his side.

"You're not ready and I can wait." Mikel said as he kissed her forehead before they both fell asleep again.

Avery sat staring at her phone. She couldn't believe that Aunt Violet canceled their dinner date for that week via text. They always had dinner on Friday night. She made her way to Dr. Williams' office and knocked on the door.

"Hey, Avery. How are you?" Harrison asked, greeting her with a big hug.

Avery gave him the side eye before having a seat. "You seem mighty jovial today," she said suspiciously.

"Really? Well, I guess that I am. Violet has reignited things in me that I thought were gone forever since Janet died." Harrison couldn't keep the smile off his face. "We are going dancing tonight. I tried to talk her into going to my cabin for the weekend, but she keeps giving me excuses as to why she can't go." Harrison sighed. "She is such an amazing woman." Avery studied Harrison while he looked off in the distance with a smile on his face. Putting two and two together, she realized what had been going on between her aunt and Harrison.

"Harrison, I have to go. I forgot that I was meeting Tonya and Alexandria for lunch. I will catch up with you later." Avery almost ran out of his office.

She dialed Violet's number. "Hey, baby girl. I'm sorry that I can't make dinner tonight. Harrison and I are going dancing. I hope that's ok." Avery noticed how happy her aunt sounded and it tugged at her heart strings. She knew that her uncle wasn't coming back and that it was time that Violet moved on with her life.

"Um, yeah, that's fine. I think that you should also go to his cabin this weekend." Avery suggested.

"But, what if you need me? I can't leave you, baby." Violet said.

"Aunt Violet, I'm 28 years old, and I can take care of myself. You don't have to protect me anymore. Enjoy yourself and your life. Uncle

Frankie isn't coming back, and you deserve to be happy. Harrison makes you happy and you make him happy. You've given up a lot to take care of me when you didn't have to." Avery felt full in her heart.

"It has been the best time of my life. I love you, baby. I'm going to call Harrison right now and tell him I'll go."

They ended the call and Avery went to the cafeteria to get a salad for lunch.

Dinner tonight. My place. Eight.

Ok. Avery texted back.

She arrived at Mikel's and rang the doorbell. Mikel answered the door and planted a kiss on Avery's lips. She petted Raven before saying, "I have something for you."

"Really, what?" Mikel asked as he walked to the kitchen.

"Not you, Raven." Avery pulled out a squeaky toy and Raven went wild. She ran in circles, causing Avery to laugh, before she sat at Avery's feet, waiting on the toy. Avery handed her the squeaky toy and Raven ran off.

"You spoil her, you know." Mikel pulled Avery close to him.

She wrapped her arms around his neck. "Yeah, I know." She kissed him before sitting at the kitchen table. "I think that your dad and my aunt are having sex."

Mikel laughed. "Yeah, probably."

"You don't find that weird?" She asked.

"Why would I?" Mikel asked as he removed the garlic bread from the oven.

"I don't know. It just seems, well..."

"Avery, you are just uncomfortable with the idea of sex in general. Once you connect on an intellectual, emotional, and spiritual level, the physical naturally comes next." He stirred the pot of pasta.

"Really, Mr. Know-it-all? Since you are such an expert on sex, where are we now? Huh?" She stood behind him, wrapping her arms around his waist.

"See, we are different. We have already connected on the intellectual, emotional, and spiritual levels, we are just gonna wait on the physical part." Mikel answered.

Avery laughed. "Oh, really?"

"Yes, really. You know that I love you, girl." Mikel blurted that last part out before he thought about it. Avery stiffened and put space between herself and Mikel. Before he could say anything to her his phone rang.

"Dammit." Mikel answered the phone. "Detective Williams. Hey, Jerry. Ok. I will be there shortly." Mikel ended the call and turned to Avery. "The food is done, go ahead and eat. I will be back as soon as I can. Don't leave. I want to talk to you."

"Ok. Do you want me to fix you a plate to take with you?" Avery asked.

"Yes, please." Mikel disappeared into his room to change his clothes.

After seeing Mikel off to work, Avery fixed herself a plate of the chicken alfredo pasta, a slice of garlic bread, and a salad. "This is pretty good, Raven." Avery broke off a piece of bread and handed it to Raven. She gobbled it up and then sat back at Avery's feet. After eating, cleaning up the kitchen, letting Raven out to do her business, and flipping through the channels on the television, she decided to shower and call it a night. Avery went into her drawer and got a pair of underwear and decided to sleep in one of Mikel's shirts because they always smelled like him. She loved the smell of him, and they brought her comfort. It was the comfort that she never thought that she would find in another human being. She looked at the clock and it said 12:30. Avery texted Mikel that she was going to bed.

The beeping of the alarm system awakened Avery. Mikel walked into the bedroom. "Hey, it's me." He kissed her on the cheek. "Are you asleep?" He asked.

"I'm up now. Are you ok?" She asked.

Mikel started taking off his clothes and put them in the dirty clothes hamper. "Nah, that was a tough one. A man killed his wife, his three children, and then himself." Mikel sighed. "This shit can really get to me at times. People are so damned evil." He said.

Avery thought to herself that she knew evil firsthand. "I know. Go ahead and shower and come to bed."

Mikel kissed her on the lips then went to shower. Avery sighed as she stared at the ceiling. Evil. She knew evil. Evil was the man that took away her Uncle Frankie. Evil was what kept her up at night. She heard the shower turn off and Mikel get out. She looked down and saw Raven asleep by the bed. She didn't move. Avery snickered thinking that Raven was no guard dog. She slept like a rock. Mikel put on his underwear in the bathroom and came to get in the bed with Avery. He stretched out his arm and Avery automatically leaned into it, snuggling against his chest.

"I'm sorry that you had to see that tonight," she said.

"It's ok. That's my job. Sometimes I wonder why I didn't just become a doctor like my pops." Avery didn't respond.

"Avery, I love you." When he felt her stiffen, he held her tighter. "You don't have to say it back, I just need to let you know that I love you."

"How do you know? You haven't known me but six months," Avery whispered.

"I'm a grown man, Avery. I know what love is, and I know that I love you. Whether it's been six months or six years, I know that I love you. I need you to know that. I want it to be me and you in this thing together." He lowered his head to look at her. "Only if you want that, too."

"There are things that you don't know about me. Things that may change your mind about wanting me and loving me," Avery answered honestly.

"Well, I want to get to know those things. We can work through them. Love never fails," Mikel countered.

"I love you too, Mikel," Avery whispered so low that Mikel couldn't hear her.

Mikel pulled her into his chest as they drifted off to sleep.

It was one of the slow days at the emergency room, so Avery was in her office, waiting until she was needed. Jeffery knocked on Avery's opened door and then entered her office. "Here are the results from those samples that you dropped off at the lab. Sorry that it took so long, I went on vacation and when I came back, they were buried on my desk at the bottom of the stack, and I completely forgot about them." Jeff handed Avery the manila envelope.

"Thanks, Jeff. That's no problem, I wasn't in a rush. I owe you one." Avery smiled.

"You have covered my ass plenty of times. This one is on the house." Jeff shut the door as he left her office.

Avery was just one of the ER doctors on staff, so her office was small, but at least she had one. She heard the code announced over the speaker and dropped the envelope on her desk and ran to the ambulance receiving area.

"Two gunshot victims. Weak pulse one, the other is DOA." The EMT said.

Avery, the other doctor on duty, and two nurses rushed the surviving patient to the first available room. They tried to stablize him, but they lost his pulse and couldn't revive him. Avery counted his gunshot wounds. There were six shots center mass. There was no way he would have survived. She saw that he had a tattoo on his neck of two guns that formed a cross. She tried to think of where she saw that before, but she was drawing a blank.

"Dr. Jones."

Avery looked up at the nurse. "Yes."

"Time of death? I need you to provide the time of death and sign off on it." She said.

"Ok." Avery looked at her watch and provided the time of death before signing off on it.

She went back to her office and sat at her desk, trying to remember where she had seen that tattoo before. She racked her brain for almost an hour, and she was still drawing a blank. She looked up when there was a knock on her opened door. It was Mikel.

"Hi, Mikel." Avery said.

"Hey, Avery. I have a few questions that I need to ask you." He responded.

His tone let her know that he was there on business and not pleasure. "Ok." Avery gave him a confused look. "About?"

"As you know, we had two homicides today, and one of the victims had this on him." Mikel showed Avery a piece of paper in a clear evidence bag with her name and address on it. "Do you know why he would have had this on him?"

"No, not at all. Do you know his name?" Avery asked.

"His name was Marcus Wainwright, A.KA. Snoop." Mikel answered.

"No, no idea." Avery perched on the side of her desk. "I did have someone go through my car earlier this week. They didn't take anything, but I guess they got my information from my registration. You think that they were after me or going to try to rob me or something?"

"Why didn't you tell me this when it happened?" Mikel asked protectively.

"I don't know. I guess it slipped my mind, Mikel. Nothing was taken, so I didn't think anything of it. It's not a big deal." Avery assured him.

"Babe, this is serious. These guys are linked to organized crime and were some heavy hitters." Mikel said.

"Dead heavy hitters." Avery reminded him.

"Avery, I'm just trying to keep you safe. I don't know what I would do if something happened to you." Mikel said.

"Nothing is going to happen to me, Mikel." Avery placed an arm around his waist.

"Just be careful, baby. Let me know if anything happens out of the ordinary. I'm going to stay at your place or you at mine until we find out what these guys were up to." Mikel insisted.

"I can take care of myself, Mikel. I promise that I will be careful." She assured him.

"Ok." He looked at his ringing phone in his hand. "I have to go, Avery. Call me when you get off. You at my place or me at yours." Mikel kissed her on the lips and headed for the door.

"Yes sir." Avery smiled and shut the door behind him. She sat at her desk and opened the envelope and then called Violet.

"Hey, sweetie. Are you on your way?" Violet was referring to their early dinner plans at her house that evening.

Avery held the contents of the envelope in her shaking hand. "When were you going to tell me that you are my mother, Adriana?"

Violet's voice shook. "Avery, listen. Just come on over baby, and we will talk about it when you get here."

"I have been grieving for you and longing for you, and you were alive this whole time. My Uncle Frankie died because of you!" Avery couldn't keep the tears from falling from her eyes.

"Avery, baby, just come home and I will explain everything to you. Please." Violet pleaded into the phone.

Avery hung up. Violet dialed her back, and it rang until she got her voicemail. She hung up and tried again. This time the phone didn't ring, it went straight to voicemail. When the doorbell rang, Violet ran to the door and opened it. She gasped and dropped the phone on the floor.

CHAPTER 12

Avery made it in her house and slammed the door behind her. She was so upset. How dare Adriana pretend to be this woman named Violet and keep her in the dark for 18 years! How dare she abandon her and then make her Uncle Frankie lie and say that she was dead! Because of her, she would never see her Uncle Frankie again. Avery stopped mid thought and it dawned on her where she had seen that tattoo before. Cleo's men had that tattoo eighteen years ago. Eighteen years ago, when they took away her Uncle Frankie. Something came over Avery, and all she felt was rage and all she could see was revenge. She called Mikel.

"Hey, Mik. What are you doing?" She asked.

"Working, baby. What's up?" Mikel answered.

Avery decided to cut straight to the chase. "Did you find out anything else about the guy that had my info? Like what he wanted, where he might have been staying? Are there any more of them?" She asked.

"Why? You trying to go hunt them down, Rambo?" Mikel laughed, but Avery didn't. "Hello?" He asked.

"Yes, I'm here." Avery answered.

LYRIC BELLAMY

"Oh. Well, we don't know much about them. The drug task force said that they came up on their radar a few months ago. As far as your safety goes, baby, you need to be careful until we can find out why a guy that was shot to death had your info on him. In fact, I'm going to place a uniform outside your house." Mikel said.

"I'm good, Mikel. That's not necessary. Thanks." Avery said. Her alarmed beeped, signaling someone was at her gate. She pulled up the camera footage and saw that two men were in a van stopped outside the gate. They were both armed with guns. She could clearly see the tattoo on the driver's neck. Two guns that formed a cross. He was one of Cleo's men.

"Mikel, I gotta go." Avery ended the call.

Mikel looked at his phone and shook his head. He loved her, but she was as stubborn as a mule at times. As soon as he got off, he would pick up Raven and then they would go to Avery's house.

Avery pushed the intercom to the gate. "May I help you?" She asked.

"I have a flower delivery for Ms. Avery Jones." The driver said.

"Ok. Just a minute." Avery said. She went into her room, changing out of her scrubs and coat, and putting on a t-shirt, light jacket, comfortable jeans, and boots. She put her knife on the inside of a hidden pocket in her jeans and a gun in her pants. She put her backup phone in the zipper of her jacket. Avery opened the gate and let them in. When the two guys made their way to the front door, they knocked on it.

"Hi, who are the flowers from?" She asked as she opened the door.

She was met by a gun being placed in her face by the driver. "Come with us, and you won't get hurt."

"Come with you where?" She raised her hands in surrender and took a few steps back inside the house. The men followed her in and shut the door.

"Listen, come with us bitch, and you will live." The driver shouted.

"Please sir, don't hurt me. Just tell me what you want." She feigned fear as she held up her hands and made tears run down her face.

"Hey man, Cleo said bring her back unharmed. Put the gun down. You see she's scared, what can she do?" The guy that was the passenger said as he put his gun back in his pants.

"Yeah, you right. But Cleo didn't tell us she would be so fine. I may get a piece of this before we drop her off." The driver put his gun on the table and walked up to Avery, placing his hand on her ass, and then squeezing. She sobbed and begged him not to hurt her.

The other man looked uncomfortable and pleaded with the driver to stop. "Hey man, this isn't what Cleo wanted us to do. He wanted us to bring her to him, that's it." He said.

"Man, take your scary ass back to the van and wait for me. I'm gonna show this bitch what it feels like to have a real man tap that ass." He ran his hands up and down Avery's trembling body.

"Whatever man." The passenger said. He walked out of the house, leaving the door partially opened, and a few moments later they heard the door slam on the van.

The driver reached under Avery's shirt and grabbed her breast. "Damn, your titties feel good." He lifted her shirt and went to dip his head to suck her breast and Avery took both hands and snapped his neck. He fell with a hard thud at her feet. Pulling down her shirt, she stepped over him to look out of the window, then went through the back door, around the house, and snuck up on the side of the van where the passenger sat with his earbuds in his ear. Avery knew that this kid was out of his element. She put the gun through the opened window and placed it to his temple.

He raised his hands in the air. "Look, I don't want any trouble. I'm just doing what I was told to do."

"Oh, you came looking for trouble when you came to my house, and you found it. Me. Now, I'm going to ask you one time, and one time only, what does Cleo want with me?" Avery said.

"I don't know. That mother fucker has lost his mind. He is in deep with some Mexican, and he has been making a lot of fucked up calls lately. We think it's money, but we don't know. He is at a warehouse waiting on us." The man answered.

"So, take me to him." She took his phone and gun, and then lowered her gun and made the man get in the driver's seat. She got in the passenger's seat and told the man to drive. Once they were on the other side of the gate, Avery instructed the man to back into it. He did as he was told, backing into the gate, leaving a dent it before driving to the warehouse. She studied the driver as he drove.

"How did you get caught up with a guy like Cleo?" She kept the gun pressed against his side.

"Fast money. I ain't got no education and no skills, so this is the only way that I can take care of my girl and two sons. Cleo recruited me at fourteen years old, and now I'm twenty-two. The streets is all I know." He answered honestly.

"That may be all you know, but you suck at it. You do know that I'm going to kill you once we make it to the warehouse, don't you?" She spoke to him honestly.

"Yeah, I know." The man continued to drive.

"What's your name and where are you from?" Avery asked.

"Quinton Blackburn, and I'm from Trejo Valley, California." He answered as he navigated the streets.

Avery looked at the young man and genuinely felt sorry for him. She felt that he was just a kid that made bad decisions, but good at heart. She pulled out her phone and typed in his info. His Facebook page popped up with his girlfriend Tameka and sons Quinton Jr. and Bryan on it. She shook her head. It always baffled her how people put all their information online for anyone and everyone to see. He pulled up to an abandoned warehouse and stopped.

"How many men are inside with Cleo?" Avery asked.

"Four, plus Cleo." He put the van in park.

"Ok, good. You are going to do as I say, and if you don't, or you decide to give away what I am going to do, I will kill Meka, little Q, and B." Avery said. She was guessing that's what their nicknames were.

Quinton bucked his eyes in disbelief. "You, you know them?"

"I know enough. Don't fuck with me, Quinton. Now deliver me to him." She ejected the magazine from his gun, emptied it, and then ejected the bullet from the chamber. She handed him the empty gun and his phone and then pocketed the bullets. "Deliver me to my father."

"Oh my God! Frankie!" Violet jumped into his arms and cried as he held her tight. "Where have you been? What are you doing here? How did you make it to the house without setting off the alarm?" She stopped talking and looked at her big brother and pulled him into another hug. "Is this real? Is this you? Please tell me it's you, Frankie."

"It is me, Adriana." He stepped into the house and closed the door behind him. She held his hand tight and led him to the couch. She couldn't stop crying.

"Shhh! Stop crying mi hermanita. I'm alive." He kissed her cheek. "I am here because we have a problem."

"What? What is it?" Violet said.

"To answer your earlier questions, you know that I set up this house and the security. That's how I made it to the front door, and I have been in California." He said.

"But I thought you were dead. We thought you were dead." She said through her creaking voice.

"That was the only way to keep you both safe, it was the only way to keep my eye on Cleo. Padre always taught us to keep your friends close-"

"But your enemies closer." Violet finished his sentence.

"Yes. Cleo thought he killed me, but Juan came back for me. He found me clinging to life and saved me. There were four of us that survived the attack, and Juan hid us all, moving us one by one to Dr. Gonzalez's clinic where he saved our lives. Juan was shot twice in the shoulder, Tank was shot in the leg and side, and Dre was shot in the hip, side, and leg. I am eternally grateful for Juan's bravery. I could not have asked for a better friend." Frankie said.

"I have to call Avery. I have to let her know that you are alive." Violet picked up her phone and started to call Avery back.

"No, that is why I am here. Cleo and his men are here. I don't know where the rest of them are hiding, but I was able to follow two of them. Today, I had to kill them. They were taken to her hospital. She will know that they are after her." Frankie said.

"Frankie, she knows who I am." Violet said.

"How?" Frankie said.

"I don't know. She called me and said…" Violet's voice trailed off. "The water bottle. I knew that she took it, but I didn't know why. She must have tested the water bottle."

"She was bound to find out, hermanita. With your hair like that, you two look just alike." Frankie ran his fingers through her short hair. "I have missed you. Te amo."

"Te amo hermano mayor." Violet couldn't believe that she had Frankie next to her. "What does Cleo want with my baby girl, Frankie?"

"From what we gather, he needs money. He has been using just as much product as he has been selling. He is in bad with his supplier again." Frankie said.

"Last time he was in that situation he promised my baby to that animal, Javier. He was really going to trade my baby to pay off a drug debt. If it wasn't for you, I don't know where my baby would be today." Violet said.

"I know, I know. That's why he sent his brother and son over to your house to take Alexandria that night all those years ago." Frankie stood and walked to the window. "I am glad that I made it in time to take care of it before they killed you. After Cleo beat you as bad as he did looking for Alexandria, I knew he had to go, too." He walked back to her and rubbed her face where the scars used to be. "You healed nicely. You almost look the same." He pulled her into another hug. "Never let a man take away the best part of you again. Padre raised us to be killers, to take care of ourselves and each other, and I raised Alex to do the same. You forgot that."

"You did a great job with her, Frankie. Thank you for that. I did a lot of things with Cleo that I wished I didn't. It took all I had not to come for her, but I knew that you could keep her safer than I ever could. Your death gave me my baby back, but it took you away. I died a little with you, Frankie." Violet said.

"And now with my life you live a little more with me." Frankie held her hand.

CHAPTER 13

"She should be here by now. She isn't answering her phone either. Frankie, something is wrong. She would have come by, even if she was mad at me." Violet started pacing the floor.

"We need to go to her." Frankie said.

They hopped in Violet's SUV, and she pulled out of her driveway in search of Avery.

They made it to Avery's house and noticed the dented gate. "Frankie, they've been here." Violet entered the gate code and it creaked open. She drove up the driveway and hopped out of her SUV. When she saw the door partially opened, she and Frankie drew their guns and cautiously approached the front door. Frankie pushed it opened a few inches more and they saw feet on the floor. They stepped inside and were relieved to see that the body wasn't Avery's. Violet lowered her gun and started to cry. "They took her."

Frankie put his gun in his pants and smiled. "No, my sweet Adriana, she took them."

"Huh?"

"She knows to never get taken. Look here. She snapped his neck with little to no effort. Nothing is out of place. There was no struggle.

Wherever she went, she went by choice." Frankie said. "Now the question is, where is she now?" Frankie wondered aloud. He searched the dead man's pockets but didn't find anything on him.

"What do we do with this piece of shit?" Violet said.

"Tarp, rope, cement blocks, lake in the back, problem solved. I'm sure she has that in the basement." Frankie said. He followed Violet to the basement and smiled as he looked around. Her basement was an exact replica of their basement in California. He went to the wall and pushed it, and the door opened. Violet watched as he walked around the basement, everything reminding him of his life with his niece and happier times. He found exactly what he was looking for in various places throughout the basement.

"I never could figure out why she brought this house so close to the lake. I guess she was waiting for this day. She has been waiting for the day to avenge your death since she was ten." Violet said.

"That is my biggest regret of being away so long. I knew that she would carry it with her, and she would want to kill Cleo, and wouldn't rest until she did." He said as they walked up the basement stairs with the items that they needed to dispose of the dead man on the floor.

They wrapped the body tight in a tarp, tying it with ropes, and Frankie rolled the dead man down the stairs to the bottom of the basement. They loaded the body and cement blocks on a cart and wheeled it through the tunnel. Opening the tunnel door, they ended up in a room in the boathouse. Loading the body in the boat, they drove out about three miles, stopped the boat, added the cement blocks, and then put the body in lake. They watched as the body quickly sank to the bottom. Driving the boat back to the boathouse, they made it back to the door, moved the door stopper, and entered the tunnel, making their way back to the house.

"Frankie, she just sent a text. It's her location." Violet said as she plugged the address into her GPS on her phone. "We have to go."

Violet grabbed her keys as she and Frankie ran to her SUV and drove to Avery's location.

"Get your ass in here." Quinton said as he pushed Avery to the ground like she told him to. She yelped and cried as she fell on her hands and knees.

Cleo sniffed a line and then walked over to Quinton and shook his hand. "Good job, Q. Where's Slim?"

"Outside taking a piss." Quinton lied.

Cleo accepted his explanation and walked over to Avery and helped her to her feet. "Don't cry, baby girl, Daddy's here," he said.

Avery snatched her arm from him. "What are you talking about? I just want to go home." She cried.

"It's true, I'm your father." Cleo said as he wiped his nose and sniffed. Avery could tell that he was high.

"No, you're not. I don't know who you think I am, but I'm not who you are looking for." Avery tried to reason with him.

"Yeah, you are. You are my little Alexandria. You would have been with me if that damn Frankie wouldn't have taken you." Cleo said.

Avery worked hard to keep her perfect façade going. "You knew my Uncle Frankie?"

"Oh, yes, I knew your Uncle Frankie. Frankie Pena." Cleo said as he started to get worked up and loud. Avery glanced around the room and saw that the four men with Cleo were not paying any attention to what was going on between the two of them. Two were playing cards, one was getting high, and the other was on the phone. She looked and saw Quinton standing in the corner, away from the rest of the guys. He wiped a tear from his eye as he typed on his phone. She thought to herself that he tried his best to keep it together, because he knew if he left or did anything out of the way, his family was as good as dead. She looked back at Cleo and listened as he continued.

"You see, I'm not perfect. I promised you to Javier when you were a baby and I owed him a lot of money." Cleo confessed. "And I did send my son and brother to Adriana's house to take you, and they did get a little rough with her, but Frankie never should have killed them. He killed my fucking brother and my only son. He didn't have to kill them. If they weren't drunk and high, they never would have tried to rape Adriana. They never would have! She should have just given you to them." Cleo tried to justify the actions of his brother and son. Avery stopped her fake crying and listened to what Cleo was saying.

"I had to push her around a little, to show her that I was serious like I had done before, but maybe I went a little too far. I wouldn't have if I wasn't high. I can still remember her face. I didn't mean to hurt her so bad. Now she is gone. I really loved her." Avery stared at him like he was insane. She took notice of his facial features, and couldn't see what Violet, or Adriana, could have possibly seen in him. He was about 5'10", medium build, dark brown skin, and average looks. He smelled like he hadn't taken a bath in a few days, and his teeth looked like he hadn't seen a dentist in years. Avery noticed that she did have his light brown colored eyes and height, but that was it. Cleo was a thug, not a drug lord. He wasn't even a good drug dealer. Everyone knew that you don't get high on your own supply. Mentally, she was disgusted by the man that stood in front of her and could not wait to kill him.

"What are you going to do to me?" Avery asked.

"Oh. I would never hurt you, baby girl." He rubbed her cheek. "You look so much like your mother." He started laughing. Avery took notice of the men again. They still were not paying any attention, no guns readily available.

"What do you want?" She whispered.

Cleo smacked his hands together. "Glad that you asked. Money. I know that your Uncle Frankie left you plenty of money when he died. I also know that you are a doctor. It took me almost twenty years to find you. That Frankie was a smart man and hid you very well. If it wasn't for Marko remembering that he saw some paperwork for a trust fund on Frankie's desk that had the name Avery Jones on it, I would have never known where to look."

"Marko?" Avery asked.

"Yes, Marko. I offered him a few grand to give me the inside scoop on you and Frankie." Cleo said.

"What happened to Marko?" Avery asked in a voice full of false fear.

"I don't know. I talked to him after I killed Frankie, but after a few months, I didn't hear from him again. Word on the street is that he got popped." Cleo was as high as a kite at this point. "I forgot the name until I ran across the paper about a year ago." Cleo had a sinister grin on his face.

"You killed my Uncle Frankie?" Avery asked like she didn't already know the answer. She just wanted to hear it from his mouth.

"Yes, I killed Frankie, but that mother fucker had it coming. But I don't want to talk about Frankie, I want to talk about the money that I need from you. I owe some people some big money and I need it from you." Cleo said.

"How much do you need?" She asked.

"One and a half million." Cleo said.

"What?" Avery was really surprised. She knew like hell Cleo was not asking her for one and half million dollars. She wouldn't give him one dollar much less that amount.

"Listen to me. Hear me out. I need that money. If I don't get the money to them soon, I'm dead. I'm your father, and that's the least you can do for me." Cleo's eyes flashed anger as he took a step closer to Avery. She took a step back.

"No," she said.

"No?" Cleo repeated.

"I said no. I won't give you the money." Avery said.

Cleo laughed and then used the back of his hand to smack Avery. She took the slap like a champ, wiping blood from the corner of her mouth. Cleo got in her face, his rancid breath almost choking her, and spoke in a tone of voice so low that only Avery could hear. "I don't think that you understand me. I'm not asking you; I'm telling you."

"And what if I still say no?" Avery asked.

"Well, then I will take it. And a little extra. Or a lot extra." Cleo shrugged and turned his back to Avery as he spoke. "And then you, my baby girl, will be reunited with your Uncle Frankie sooner rather than later."

Avery looked around one last time at the four men in the room. They were oblivious to the fact that they were about to meet their demise. She looked at Quinton who was still away from the group, staring at her, knowing that he was about to die. She pulled her gun and made five perfect shots, watching each of the men hit the floor of the warehouse. When Cleo turned around, he came face to face with a piece of smoking steel pointed at his head.

CHAPTER 14

IIIIIIIIIIIIIIIIIIIIIIIIIIIIIIIIIIIIIIIIIIIIIIIIIIIIIIIIIIIIIIIIIIIIIIIIIIIIIIIIIII

"**O**h shit. What you think you doing, you little bitch?" Cleo said.

"Move." She pointed towards the area of the building where the tables were set up and the men lie dead on the floor.

Cleo followed her directions, walking to the back of the abandoned warehouse. "What's your plan, baby girl? You gonna kill your old man?"

"First off, you're nothing to me. Secondly, yes, I am going to kill you. You see, the day that you killed my Uncle Frankie is the day that you signed your death warrant. You think that I'm this sweet little girl who will fold and bend to you because you slap me. I was taking on grown men when I was 10. See, my Uncle Frankie raised me to be a killer when I had to be, and I won't even flinch when I pull the trigger to kill you." She punched Cleo in his face, followed by a punch to his side and a strike to his throat. Cleo fell to his knees and grabbed his throat, gasping for air.

"You little bitch! I'm gonna kill your ass." He said as he gasped for air.

"Nah, Dad, that won't happen. Today is the day that you die." She aimed the gun at his head and put her finger on the trigger, when she heard the front door open. She stepped to the side, keeping her gun on Cleo, and glanced towards the door.

"Alexandria, wait, baby." Violet said as she ran towards Avery.

"This doesn't concern you." Avery said, her eyes still on Cleo.

Cleo's eyes bucked in surprise. "Adriana?"

"Fuck you, Cleo!" She kicked him in his face, and then kicked him twice in his side.

"Mi corazón." Frankie walked into the door and towards Avery.

Avery furrowed her brow before looking towards the front door. She thought that her eyes were playing tricks on her. She blinked four times before she realized that she was staring at a face that she longed to see for the last eighteen years. "Uncle Frankie?" Avery asked in a confused voice.

"Yes, it's me, Alexandria. It's me, mi corazon." Frankie walked towards her.

She looked at Violet and then at Cleo on the floor crying like a baby, mumbling something about Adriana and Frankie being back from the dead and him losing his mind. She turned and ran to Frankie, hugging him tight. She cried in his arms.

"Uncle Frankie. Where have you been? I've missed you. I love you so much! Why didn't you come back for me?" She couldn't hold back her sobs.

"Shhh, shhhh, mi corazón. I have missed you, too. The only way to keep you safe was to keep you away. I love you so much, mi corazón. I've missed you so much." He kissed her cheek. "The haircut suits you. You look just like your mother." He ran his hand through her short curls.

She hugged him tight again. "I'm never letting you go again, Uncle Frankie."

"You don't have to," he said. He looked around at all the bodies on the floor and asked. "Your work?"

"Yeah, mine. Oh, one second," she said as she walked over to Quinton.

Violet stood by Frankie and watched as Avery kicked Quinton's foot. Suddenly, she saw Cleo reach for a gun on the table. She heard her uncle's words replay in her mind, only this time they were bittersweet.

Center mass. Go.

Pulling the trigger she executed four perfect shots center mass.

Head shots. Go.

She pulled the trigger once more sending a bullet to the center of his head. She looked into his eyes as they went lifeless and his body hit the floor. She stared at him for a few seconds, hoping to feel something for the man who was responsible for her existence. Feeling nothing, she shrugged and turned back to Quinton.

"Get your ass up. I know you aren't dead." Avery laughed.

Quinton moaned and tried to sit up. "It burns and hurts like a mother fucker," he said.

"Yeah, I know, but be thankful that you aren't like your friends over there." Avery moved to the side so that he could see the dead bodies. She put her gun in her waistband and offered her hand to him, helping him up.

"What's the guy's name that came to my house with you?" Avery asked Quinton.

"Slim." Quinton said.

"I know that. His real name? Come on, we don't have all day," she said.

"Um, Simon Daniels."

"Ok, so, this is what you are going to do. You are going to call 911 and tell them that you've been shot, and you need help. When they get here, you don't know what happened. You are here from California visiting your cousin who lives in the projects with his girl-friend named Pooh, and he said that he needed to make a stop. You can pick anyone of these dead guys to be your cousin, they can't say otherwise." Avery laughed a little. "You don't know anything other than some guys came in and had some words with Cleo there and then they started blasting." She looked at him. "Now, they are going to ask why you weren't executed like the rest of them. You tell them that you backed away and started to run, and when they shot you, you played dead. Sell it. Make it seem real. Cry, throw up, piss on yourself if you have to. You don't have one of those tattoos, do you?"

"No, I haven't earned them yet." Quinton said.

"Good. Now, when they release you, go home and get your ass off the streets, get your GED, go to trade school or college, and make something of yourself. Your children deserve better. And marry Meka. But, if you ever tell anyone what happened I will kill you, your girlfriend, and your two sons. You know that I'm good for it. You've never seen me, you don't know my name, and you don't know where I live. Got it?" Avery said.

Quinton started to shake a little. "Got it," he answered.

Avery took his phone and gun. He only had $24 in his pocket. She handed him a burner phone to call 911 and told him that she would get rid of his phone and gun for him because she knew that he had some incriminating information in it.

"Ma'am, why didn't you kill me?" He asked.

"Should I have?" She raised her gun to his head, and he pissed in his pants.

"No, no, no ma'am," he stuttered.

"Good." She walked over to her mother and Uncle Frankie. "Let's go home."

Violet drove to Avery's house as Avery sat in the back with Frankie.

"Are you sure letting him go was the right decision? I would have killed him along with the others." Frankie said.

Avery held his hand and placed her head on his shoulder. "It was absolutely the right decision. I have learned to read people, and he deserved a second chance." She looked at their intertwined hands and smiled.

"Avery, I'm so sorry that I didn't tell you that I was your mother." Violet said.

Avery didn't respond, she just continued to focus on the pair of intertwined hands. Love. She had her Uncle Frankie back.

"I swore Frankie to secrecy, to never tell you that I was alive. I was never in the car that went over the cliff. Him raising you was my only option and only way to keep Cleo from taking you." Violet continued. "I was going to tell you, and soon. I wanted to tell Harrison too, but I was just waiting for the right moment. I'm sorry, but I don't regret doing it for one minute. I just wanted to ask how did you know? Was it the water bottles?"

"Who is Harrison?" Frankie asked protectively.

"He's her boyfriend," Avery responded. "Yes. It was also your hair cut. I always figured that you weren't black, that you were biracial, but I didn't put two and two together until I saw you with your hair cut short. I have your chin and your cheekbones. My nose is just a slight variation of yours, but we look just alike."

"I had reconstructive surgery done on my nose after the last time Cleo put his hands on me. It was broken so badly and in so many places that they had to almost make me another nose, while attempting to make me look the same. Testing the water bottles was smart." Violet looked in her rearview mirror at Avery.

"Yeah. So, what now? Do I call you mom, Aunt Violet, Adriana? How does this work?" Avery asked.

Frankie answered for her. "We will cross that bridge when we come to it." Frankie kissed Avery on her forehead. "I have missed you so much, mi corazon. The old part of my life is over. I am never going away again."

"I love you, Uncle Frankie." Avery held his hand tight as they rode in silence to her house.

After making it to her house, Avery walked in and turned in circles looking for the Simon's body.

"We handled it," Frankie said.

"Thanks." She picked up her cellphone and saw that she had four missed calls from Mikel. She dialed his number back.

"Avery, are you ok?" He asked.

"Yes, I'm fine. I was outside getting the information from the guy that accidentally backed into my gate. Are you ok? What's wrong?" She asked as she noticed he sounded like he was in a rush.

"Yeah, I was just checking on you. I'm headed to a call now. I will be by after work. Keep your doors locked and don't answer the door for anyone." Mikel demanded.

"Yes, sir."

Mikel automatically smiled and laughed. "I will see you later, baby." He ended the call and headed to the crime scene at an abandoned warehouse.

Avery went into the living room with her uncle and mother and took a seat next to her Uncle Frankie. "So, how do we tell Mikel and Harrison?" she asked before she made a face. "How can mother and daughter date father and son? That's weird?"

"Who is Mikel?" Frankie asked.

"He is Harrison's son, and sort of my boyfriend," Avery said, suddenly bashful. "But we have not had sex. I have kept every promise that I made to you." She smiled and placed her head on her uncle's shoulder.

"Hmm," he said.

"Hmm what?" Avery looked at him. Violet watched the two interact with a smirk on her face. It was like they had never been apart; he was still the uncle that she respected, admired, and obeyed.

"A boyfriend. I know that you are a grown woman, but I have a tough time accepting that you have grown up without me," Frankie admitted.

"Well, I always had you with me." She opened the locket and Frankie smiled. "I think that you will like him. He is a detective."

Frankie raised his eyebrows in surprise.

"Yeah, I know, but he does all that he can to make me happy and protect me. Like you." She smiled admiringly at her uncle again.

"Well, I think that I need to meet this, Mikel," Frankie responded.

"Well, first, I need to explain to him that you are alive." Avery's phone rang before she could finish talking. She answered it. "Ok. I will be there shortly." She placed her phone in her lap. "The hospital needs me; they are short staffed. Do you mind?" she asked Frankie.

"No, mi corazon. Go ahead. I will stay at Adriana's tonight. We will get together tomorrow." He stood and hugged her tight.

"I miss you already." The tears escaped her eyes.

"Alexandria, it's only for a few hours. You know where to find me. I'm not going anywhere." He laughed and looked into her sweet brown eyes as if she was still ten years old. He broke their embrace so that she could get ready for work.

"We will see you later, Avery," Violet said.

Avery hugged her tight, catching her off guard. "Ok, Mom."

Violet returned her embrace. "I have longed to hear those words for 28 years. I love you, Alexandria."

"And I love you. Thank you for everything." Avery stepped back and led the two of them to the front door.

She shut the door and smiled, feeling a sense of ease and security. Avery had her Uncle Frankie back. She had a mother. She killed Cleo. Everything came full circle for her. She had never lost the most important people in her life; they were all still with her. She smiled as she showered and gathered her things before leaving for work.

CHAPTER 15

"This guy was a hell of a shot," Detective Murano said as he knelt to look at the victim laying on the dusty warehouse floor.

Mikel took in the entire scene before him. "Yeah, he sure was." Mikel felt like something was missing. Like the scene told a story, but not the entire story. He turned to the other detective. "I'm going to go and talk to the surviving witness." Detective Murano nodded to Mikel as he continued processing the scene. Mikel walked outside to the ambulance to speak to the witness. The paramedics were patching him up before taking him to the hospital.

"I'm Detective Williams," Mikel said. "What happened in there?"

"I already told the other detective everything that I know." Quinton winced in pain.

"I know, but now I need you to tell me."

Quinton sighed. "Ok. I will tell you everything."

Making her rounds, Avery knocked on the door before entering.

"Please don't kill me, ma'am. I did what you told me to do. I said everything that you told me to say." Quinton started to cry.

"Boy, stop crying. I know. I'm here to help you." Avery assured him. She removed a stack of bills from her coat pocket, put them in a white catalog envelope, and then handed it to him. "You have twenty thousand dollars in here. Take a bus home. Move your family somewhere safe. Go to school and give your sons the chance that you didn't have." She handed him some papers. "I am discharging you. Sign these papers and take this set of papers with you. It's your prescription and some info on your wound care. Put them in the envelope. It will look like it contains your discharge papers, and no one will know about the money. Now, you can go," Avery said as she stood.

"Thank you," he whispered.

"You can thank me by being a better you. Now go ahead and get out of here."

Quinton got dressed as fast as he could and exited the room. Avery delivered the papers to the discharge desk and went to her office. She texted Mikel and told him that she was headed back home. Once she was home and showered, then crawled into bed and texted her Uncle Frankie. He texted her back and she smiled. She could admit that she was exhausted. As soon as she closed her eyes, Mikel called to let her know that he was at the gate. Avery let him through the gate and hugged him tight once he and Raven made it into the house.

"What's that for?" he asked as he planted a kiss on her lips.

"I just needed to hug you," she said.

Mikel smiled at her. "Thank you. I needed a hug. I just left one of the worst crime scenes I have ever been to. Bodies everywhere."

Avery eased out of his arms and took his bag out of his hands. "Are you hungry?"

"Nah. I just need a shower and you," he answered honestly.

Avery smiled back, taking his bag into her room and not the guest room. Mikel followed her. "What happened tonight?" she asked.

"Some drug dealer owed some money to the wrong person. He killed him and his crew. The only survivor was a guy that ran. Poor fella." Mikel said, removing his shirt. "My boss wants us to not waste any more resources or time on it. All the dead guys had rap sheets a mile long, ranging from robbery to murder. The ways he sees it, live by the sword, die by the sword, but I think something is missing. Something doesn't feel right about it." Mikel shook his head. "The survivor was scared shitless. Pissed himself and everything."

"Oh, goodness. He was scared." Avery said as she helped him out of his shoes and socks.

"Yeah. And you know, all the dead guys had those tattoos." Mikel told Avery, trying not to become aroused by her undressing him.

"What tattoos?" She said as she unbuckled his pants while staring into his eyes.

Mikel let out a shaky breath. No woman has ever affected him the way Avery did. "The tattoos that the guy had that we found your address on." He said.

"Oh, that tattoo." Avery nonchalantly said as she reached for his boxers. They had never seen each other naked, but tonight would be the exception.

Mikel's member stood erect as Avery looked at it. She wanted to touch him, but she didn't. She grabbed his hand and led him into her bathroom and turned on her shower. Mikel marveled at her bathroom. It was fit for royalty. Avery pushed the buttons on the side of the shower and then turned to Mikel.

"The water is just like you like it." She stepped back so that Mikel could enter the oversized Roman shower equipped with four shower heads, each spraying water from a different direction.

Mikel gazed down at Avery and reached for the bottom of her shirt. He pulled it above her head with no resistance from her. With her shirt removed, he finally saw her perfect breasts in all their glory. He removed her shorts and panties before grabbing her hand and guiding her into the shower with him. No words were spoken between them as the water kneaded all his stress away. Avery reached for the shampoo and lathered up his hair. He leaned back to rinse away the shampoo as Avery kissed his chest. Mikel lathered up her soft curls with shampoo and she turned to rinse her hair. She felt his large erection against her back. She was too mesmerized to move. Mikel reached for her body wash and started to lather her shoulders and then reached down to her breasts. Lathering them both, he tweaked her nipples between his fingers and got rock hard as she moaned. Mikel turned her around to face him. He dipped his head and placed his lips to hers. When she slipped her tongue in his mouth, he picked her up, and she wrapped her legs around his waist. There, under the shower, Mikel wanted to make love to her. He wanted to show her how much he loved her, but he didn't. He broke the kiss and held her tight.

"I love you so much, Avery." He told her as he looked in her eyes.

She smiled. "Do you now?" She teased.

"Hell yeah, I do. I think that this is as far as we go tonight. As bad as I want to make love to you tonight, right her in this shower, I want our first time, your first time, to be something that you will never forget." Avery had made him soft. Any other time with any other woman, he would have hit it in the shower without hesitation, but not Avery. He could never do that to her.

"Ok." She said before planting another passionate kiss on his lips.

Avery was the first to exit the shower. She dried herself and then went in search of Raven. As Avery thought, she was in her dog bed, fast asleep. Avery laughed as she set the alarm and turned off the lights, leaving on a light in the hallway.

That night, they held each other tight as they drifted off to sleep. Something shifted in their relationship, and they both liked it. Avery didn't tell him that she loved him, but Mikel knew that she did. He knew that she wanted to be with him as much as he wanted to be with her. The next morning, after their morning run, Avery called the gate company to come repair her gate and she and Mikel went to the lake. She sat in his lap on the wicker sofa.

"I have never felt as complete as I do now." Mikel said.

"Neither have I." Avery said. She had been thinking of a way to tell Mikel about her true identity. She felt like he deserved to know who she really was. "Mikel, will you love me no matter what?"

Mikel felt like he was punched in the stomach. "Yes, baby. I love you, and I will love you no matter what, but please don't tell me that there is someone else." Mikel held his breath as he waited for her to answer.

"No, nothing like that." Avery sighed and then wrapped her arms around his neck. "Let's drop Raven off at your place and go and get something to eat."

Mikel kissed her. "Ok."

Avery had never been so unsure of something in her life. She was supposed to bring Mikel over to Violet's after dinner so that he and Frankie could meet. She didn't know how the meeting would go or how she would tell him everything, but she knew that she had to.

After dropping Raven off, they went to eat an early dinner. As usual, they were their best selves when they were together and there was no feeling in the world better than they felt at that moment.

"I know we talked about this briefly before, but I will ask again. Marriage and kids. Is that something that you never want, you don't want right now, or something that you have always dreamed of?" Mikel asked.

Avery thought for a moment. "Honestly, I have never really put much thought into it, but I love the idea of a family. I never had a mother or a father, only my uncle and my aunt, and now I guess I would love to have a traditional family one day. Me, my husband, and our three kids." She said.

"That's what's up." Mikel nervously fidgeted in his pocket. He felt the ring that he bought a month ago, thinking that it was foolish then, but now knowing now that he made the right decision. Tonight, was going to be the night that he asked Avery to marry him. He couldn't go another day without her officially being his.

"I know that you want what your parents had. You talk about it all the time." Avery said as she finished off her glass of tea.

"I do. I want to be as happy as they were and raise a family of children just like me." Mikel said.

"Lord help their momma." Avery laughed.

"There is only one woman that I have ever thought about starting a family with, and she is going to be my wife." Mikel countered.

"Oh, really." Avery said, biting back the jealousy that started rising within her.

"Yep. And she is everything-" Mikel was cut off by a woman stopping next to their table.

"Hey Mikel." The lady stood at their table in a tight black jump-suit, six-inch heels, and a weave down to her butt. The lady looked as if she was ready to eat Mikel alive.

Mikel turned and looked at her. He couldn't remember her name, but he did remember that she was crazy as hell. "Oh, hey Gwen." Mikel said before turning his attention back to Avery.

"It's Denise. So now you don't remember me? You gave me a night I could never forget." She giggled and licked her lips suggestively.

"Obviously you just weren't worth remembering." Avery quipped.

Mikel laughed hard. Denise looked Avery up and down with her nose turned up in the air like she smelled something rotten.

"And you are?" Denise asked.

"Someone who he will never forget." She grabbed Mikel's hand from across the table. "Are you ready to go, baby?" She asked.

Impressed, Mikel smirked and responded. "I sure am, babe. Good seeing you again, Denise."

Mikel left the bill and the tip on the table, took Avery's hand in his, and started for the door. On the way out, Mikel spotted one of his fellow officers, Marcus, waiting to be seated. After introducing Avery to Marcus and his wife, and conversing for a few minutes, Mikel and Avery walked towards Mikel's SUV.

"Oh, so I won't forget you, huh?" Mikel asked.

"Nope." Avery said as she walked a few steps ahead of Mikel.

She turned just in time to see the gun pointed to the back of Mikel's head.

"Give me the keys mother fucker. And your wallet." The assailant ordered. He wore all black with a bandana covering his nose and mouth.

"I'm a police officer, man. You don't want to do this." Mikel countered.

"A cop? Man, fuck you." They guy pulled the trigger, and Avery heard the click.

Immediately she sprang into action, disarming the assailant, and sending him flying to the ground with a broken nose before Mikel could even turn around.

"You have the safety on, genius." Avery said as she took the safety off and pointed the gun at his head. Her heart was beating wildly as adrenaline raced through her body. She almost shot the guy in the head for the simple fact that he attempted to take Mikel's life.

Mikel flipped him over on his stomach and told Avery to keep her foot on his back, so he couldn't get up. Mikel found some plastic ties in his SUV that he could use to subdue him until a uniform arrived. He started to tie the guy's hands when he and Avery both saw a car barreling towards them, the driver was in the same clothing as the guy on the ground. Avery heard the shots before she could fully turn around to react and felt a burn in both her left shoulder and side, and she instantly knew that bullets were the cause of her pain. She turned and went to fire at the car while the driver was leaning out of the window, but she felt like her body was on fire, feeling two more bullets rip through her body

"Avery, get down!" Mikel demanded as he stood to pull her to the ground.

Quickly pulling herself together, with one shot, she put a bullet in the driver's head. He instantly slumped over the steering wheel, as his car collided with a parked car in the parking lot. Marcus immediately drew his gun and ran to the parking lot when he heard the shots. He saw a car crashed into a parked car, a man on the ground with his hands tied behind his back, and Mikel on the ground, covered in blood and cradling Avery as she struggled to breathe.

"Mikel, are you hit?" Marcus asked as he keep his gun trained on the car while he approached.

"No, it's not my blood. She needs an ambulance!" Mikel called back.

After Marcus saw that they driver was lifeless, and his gun on the ground, he ran back to Mikel and Avery. They could hear the sirens and looked around to see the police in the parking lot. Marcus waved them over, flashed his ID, picked the man up off the ground and put him in the back of the first police car.

"Avery, come on baby, stay with me. Help is almost here. They are almost here, baby. Avery! Open your eyes, baby. Open your eyes!" Mikel was franticly trying to keep Avery alert. She tried to speak, but only spit up blood. The paramedics removed Avery from Mikel's arms and placed her on the stretcher. Mikel ran behind them, jumping into the back of the ambulance with Avery. He sat back and watched as they worked to stabilize her.

"Weakening pulse." One paramedic said to the other as she cut off Avery's shirt and placed a needle in her chest while the other paramedic started an IV.

They continued to work on Avery while Mikel watched until he couldn't watch anymore. He called his father to let him know what happened and told him to contact Violet so that she could meet them at the hospital. Mikel did his best to answer the questions that the paramedics asked as they made their way to the hospital.

"She's a doctor here at Memorial hospital. Let them know that. I'm a police officer and I need to be with her." Mikel said.

The paramedics relayed the message to the waiting ER staff at the hospital. They pulled into the hospital, and they were met with all the available medical staff. Mikel was barely out of the ambulance before around twenty people whisked her away and shouted instructions to each other. Mikel tried to follow them, but he was stopped but a nurse.

"Sir, you can't go back there." The nurse said.

"I have to be with her." Mikel added.

"I understand sir, but we have it from here. I can assure you that we will do all we can to save Dr. Jones' life." The nurse placed a hand on Mikel's shoulder, and Mikel noticed that it trembled. It was clear to him that Avery was cared about a great deal at this hospital.

"Ok. Just please let me know how she is." Mikel said. He turned when he heard Harrison yell his name.

He ran to his dad and Harrison pulled him into a hug. Mikel cried on his father's shoulder. "Pops, I don't know if she will make it."

"She will son, she will." Harrison assured him.

"I need you to go check on her." Mikel said.

"I am. I just want to wait on Violet." As if Harrison conjured her up with his words, Violet found Harrison and Mikel and ran to them followed by a Hispanic male.

"Harrison, is she ok? Is my baby going to be ok?" Violet yelled as she cried and trembled.

"I'm going to check and see. You know that we will do all that we can, honey." Harrison held her tight.

Mikel eyed the Hispanic male suspiciously as he stood back with tears in his eyes. The unknown man wiped his tears and Mikel noticed he was trying to get his breathing under control. Mikel decided to speak up. "Sir, this is a private moment, can you stand somewhere else?"

Harrison was the first to speak. "Mikel, he is family. Why don't you go to my office and wash up? I should have a clean shirt there. I will let security know that you are coming."

"Who the hell is he?" Mikel asked.

"We will talk about this later. Go and change. I will go and make sure Avery is ok." Harrison ordered Mikel this time. Mikel took his father's keys and sprinted to the elevator.

"Harrison, you have to save my baby. I can't lose her." Violet begged.

"We can't lose her." Frankie added. He felt like he was dying each second that he didn't know how Avery was. He started to shake and took a seat in the private waiting area that Harrison escorted them to. "Harrison, she is my heart. Please help her, senor." Frankie said as he clasped his shaking hands in his lap.

"You have my word, Frankie. You both have my word." Harrison turned to Violet. "I love you, honey, and I will make sure that we all do our best to make sure she pulls through."

"I love you, too. And I know you will." Violet kissed Harrison on his lips and took the seat next to Frankie.

When Harrison exited the waiting room, he saw Mikel coming down the hall. He showed Mikel where to wait and then he went back to check on Avery.

Mikel took the seat opposite Frankie and Violet. He noticed that they held hands while they talked. He looked from Violet to Frankie and back from Frankie to Violet. Avery's opened locket flashed in Mikel's mind, and he saw the picture. The picture of the man that sat across from him, only younger. Anger surged through Mikel as he thought that Violet was cheating on his father with her ex, Frankie.

"Uncle Frankie?" Mikel asked.

Frankie turned to Mikel. "Si."

"Avery said you were dead. And Violet, are you cheating on my dad with your ex? You have some damn nerve. Family my ass!" Mikel raised his voice as he spoke to Frankie only. "Avery thought that you were dead. What kind of shit is this? You are having an affair while my woman fights for her life?" Mikel stood and covered the space between himself and Frankie.

Frankie stood and faced Mikel. Frankie was older but was still in great shape and could take Mikel down with one strike if he needed to. Violet stood between the two of them.

"Mikel, it's not what you think." Violet said.

"Well, what is it?" Mikel yelled as he stared Frankie down. He knew that he was being irrational, and his anger was displaced, but he didn't care.

"Mikel, sit your ass down now!" Violet ordered, and he reluctantly obeyed.

"Frankie isn't my ex, he is my brother." Violet said as she sighed and wiped her brow with shaking fingers. This was all too much for her. She and Frankie told Mikel everything about the family, past to present, leaving out the parts about the man that Avery killed in her home, Cleo's murder, and the fact that he was Avery's father. Mikel sat there and listened in disbelief. If what he was hearing was true, Avery wasn't who he thought she was. Everything made sense now. All the security, her skills, the way that she made a perfect head shot today after being shot four times herself. He didn't know anyone that could have made that shot. The gears started turning in Mikel's head.

The return of Uncle Frankie coincided with the deaths of the guys with tattoos. When they had finished their story, Mikel went ahead and asked about the murders.

"I found Avery's name and address on a guy that was brought into this hospital. He was murdered, and so was the guy he was with. Did you do that?" Mikel asked.

"Yes. I had to protect my baby girl, and I would do it again." Frankie answered.

"And the warehouse?" Mikel asked.

Violet and Frankie looked at each other but didn't say a word.

"It was Avery, wasn't it?" Mikel asked.

They both stared at him, neither confirming nor denying his accusations.

Mikel laughed. He couldn't believe what he was hearing. He reached into his pocket and pulled out the ring. "I had planned on talking to you tonight, and then asking Avery to marry me. I love her more than anything, and now she could possibly lose her life trying to protect me. She is so damned stubborn. All she had to do was get down." Mikel's hands started to shake, and his voice cracked.

"You have my blessing," Frankie said.

"And mine." Violet added.

"But what if-" Mikel couldn't finish the sentence.

All three of their heads turned towards the door as it opened. Mikel could read his father's face. It was the same look that he had when he told him and his brother that their mother was dying.

"No. No. No! Don't you fucking say it!" Mikel stood and started backing towards the wall.

Violet looked at Mikel and then at Harrison. "Harrison?" She said.

Harrison sighed. "We have done all that we can do. The rest is up to Avery. We just have to wait and see what happens."

"My baby! Lord, please save my baby!" Violet yelled as she cried and almost crumbled to the floor. Frankie caught her and guided her to the chair.

"Hermana, she will make it. She is stronger than you and me both." Frankie took the seat next to her.

Harrison kneeled in front of Violet and whispered something in her ear. Violet nodded her head and then Harrison walked over to Mikel.

"Son." Harrison placed his hand on Mikel's shoulder.

Mikel looked at his father with tears streaming down his face. "Pops, I can't lose her, too."

A lump formed in Harrison's throat as he pulled his son into a hug. A knock on the door caused them all the stare in the direction of the door like Avery would just walk through it at any moment. After a minute of complete silence, Harrison opened the door. A police officer stood in the doorway.

"Hello, sir. I was looking for Detective Williams." The officer said.

Mikel stepped forward. "What's up, Larry?"

"I'm sorry to hear about everything. I just wanted to let you know that the perp that we have in custody said that it was a gang initiation. He was supposed to rob and kill you and your girlfriend and bring the truck back. Chief is on his way here to the hospital. We have SWAT headed to the drop house. We are going to nail these bastards." The officer stated confidently, displaying the camaraderie that was common among them all.

"I appreciate it, man." Mikel and Larry shared the handshake and one arm embrace that all men did. With all that happened so quickly,

Mikel forgot about the circumstances that led them to their current situation. All he thought about was Avery.

"No problem, man. Keep us posted on Dr. Jones." Larry said before exiting the room.

Mikel faced his father and asked a question that he didn't really want to know the answer to. "How bad is it?"

Harrison sighed and looked at Violet and Frankie before focusing his attention back on Mikel. "Two bullets went straight through her body, one is too close to her spine to remove, and the one that we did remove caused her lung to collapse."

"Is she going to make it?" Mikel knew he sounded hopeful.

"She is obviously a fighter, and I think she will pull through. She could have died with the collapsed lung alone, but she didn't." Harrison said.

"Yes, she is a fighter." Frankie echoed.

Mikel, Violet, and Frankie all sat in her room. The hospital bent the rules for them and let them stay as long as they wanted, which was all day every day for the past week and a half. The beeping of the machines almost drove Mikel insane. Frankie stood at her side and stroked her hair as he spoke to her in Spanish. She was taken off the ventilator that morning, but she had a tube in her nose. Avery still did not wake up. Harrison entered the room. He kissed Violet, shook Frankie's hand, and then hugged Mikel.

"She has made a lot of improvement. We are just waiting for her to wake up." He poked and prodded her as he spoke. "Why don't you guys go and get something to eat and get some rest. I will be here to check in on her."

"I'm not leaving, Pops." Mikel continued staring at Avery. She looked nothing like herself. She looked tired and pale.

"Son, you haven't had more than a few minutes of sleep here and there for the past ten days. Quite frankly, you look and smell like shit." This made Violet and Frankie laugh a little. "Go home, eat, and get some sleep. I'm not asking you, I'm telling you." Harrison said.

Violet and Frankie said their goodbyes to Avery, promising to come back, and then their goodbyes to Harrison and Mikel. Mikel hugged his father, kissed Avery and whispered in her ear before heading home. Once he was in his truck, he sniffed under his arms and winced. He did smell bad. After stopping at a drive thru and making it home to shower, he got into bed. He was thankful that his brother took Raven to his house and was watching her while he was in the hospital with Avery. Mikel set his alarm for an hour and closed his eyes. When he woke up, he grabbed his phone and saw that it was eight in the morning. He had slept for eleven hours. He jumped out of bed, got dressed, and rushed to the hospital. When he made it back to the room, Frankie was there with Avery.

"You must have gotten some much needed rest. You look much better." Frankie stood and shook Mikel's hand.

"Yes. I wanted to be back before now. I guess I was more tired than I wanted to admit." Mikel rubbed the back of his neck and walked over to Avery and kissed her on the lips. "I love you, baby. Please come back to me." There was no response from Avery. Mikel turned to Frankie. "Has there been any change?"

"None. But do not fear, she will pull through." Frankie offered a smile to Mikel.

Mikel took a seat next to Frankie and pulled up his work emails as a distraction from the constant beeping that threatened his sanity. He was glad to see that Cleo's case was closed, just like his boss wanted. No more questions would be asked. The raid was successful on the gang that was responsible for Avery's shooting. They arrested 20 men, including the leader. Some snitched, some didn't, but they had enough evidence to put them all behind bars for a very long time. Mikel looked up from his phone when he heard Avery groan. Frankie ran to her side, but Mikel was frozen in his seat as he heard the beeping grow louder.

"Where is he?" Avery whispered.

"I'm here, mi corazon. I'm here." Frankie rubbed her hair.

"Mikel?" Avery struggled to open her eyes. Hearing his name brought Mikel out of his trance as he ran to her side. The door opened, and the nurses and doctors rushed in.

Avery became more upset, and the monitors went wild. "Mikel. Where is he? I need to know that he is alive." She choked on her words as she began to cry. Her throat was raspy and sore, and her chest ached.

"I'm right here, baby." Mikel stroked her head as the nurses and doctors smiled with relief as they checked her and the monitors.

"I thought you died. I. I love you." Avery whispered and tried to reach for Mikel but winced in pain.

"I'm here, baby. I will always be right here. Calm down. Calm down." Mikel tried to calm her down.

The doctors eased in and started to talk to Avery, seeing if she was coherent enough to understand what they were saying and updating her on her condition.

"Are you in much pain?" The doctor asked.

"Yes, Jeff, I am, but I do not want any medication right now. I need some time alone with my family first. And please remove this tube before I do it myself." Avery all but demanded. Her throat was raw and her voice raspy, but she forced every word out of her throat.

Frankie laughed. She was back to herself, and well on the road to recovery. Once everyone finally exited the room, Avery looked from Mikel to Frankie.

"Mikel, there are some things that I need to tell you." Avery went to move and winced in pain again.

Mikel and Frankie were instantly at her side. Avery laughed and turned to Frankie.

"Bullets hurt like a bitch!" She laughed again, and Frankie leaned down to kiss her on her forehead.

"Yes, they do. I will let you two talk." Frankie started to leave, but Avery grabbed his hand.

"You don't have to go. Please stay, Uncle Frankie."

"Mi corazon, you don't need me anymore. You have this nice young man now to protect you." Frankie nodded towards Mikel.

"I will always need you, Uncle Frankie. Always." As Avery spoke, a lone tear escaped her eyes and ran down her cheek. Frankie wiped away the tear and kissed her on her cheek.

"I love you more than life itself, Alexandria. Talk to Mikel now. I will be in the hallway." With that, Frankie exited the room and Avery turned back to Mikel.

Mikel poured Avery a cup of water and let her take a sip. She cleared her throat. "I don't know how to say what I need to say, so I guess I will just say it." Avery released the breath she was holding.

"I already know, baby. Your uncle and mom told me everything." Mikel gently sat next to her on the bed.

Avery's eyes bucked with surprise. "Everything?"

"Yes. Well, I filled in the blanks on some parts. Baby, why didn't you just tell me?" Mikel ran his hands through her short curls.

"Mikel, I was going to. That's what I wanted to do the night that we were attacked. Were they Cleo's men?" Avery asked.

"No, some gang initiation." Mikel answered.

"I see." Avery relaxed a little before she began speaking again. "You know what's crazy? You have sworn to uphold the law, and I broke it. I come from a line of law breakers, drug dealers, and worse. I understand if this is where our relationship ends. But I want you to know that I love you." She smiled and Mikel smiled back. "Yeah, I said it. I love you. You are the only man I have ever loved other than my Uncle Frankie." Avery opened her hand for Mikel to place his hand in hers.

"You deserve more than me. We will never work. I am who I am. A killer. A liar. I am Alexandria Pena."

"You may be all those things, but don't forget that you're also a brilliant doctor that saves lives every day. You are thoughtful, funny, beautiful, and not to mention unbelievably sexy. And you're the woman I love and want to spend the rest of my life with." Mikel reached in his pocket and pulled out the ring that he thought he may never be able to give to Avery. He walked over to the left side of the bed, kneeled on one knee, and took her hand in his.

"I love you, Avery Jones or Alexandria Pena, whichever you want me to call you. No matter what happens in life, whatever storms we may face, I want to spend each waking day with you. I want to spend every day protecting and loving you like a husband should. Will you be my wife? Will you marry me?" Mikel's voice shook along with his hands as he proposed to Avery.

"But what about-."

"There are no what abouts. All I'm asking is if you want to spend the rest of your life with me. I love my job, but it's not coming between us. Believe it or not, I did get accepted into medical school before joining the force. It's always an option." Mikel offered Avery one of his charming smiles.

"Yes." She answered.

"Yes?"

"Hell yes!" Avery's laugh turned into a cough as Mikel placed the ring on her finger and kissed her gently on her lips.

"Oh, baby. I love you so much." Mikel continued to plant gentle kisses on her lips.

"And I love you." Avery could admit that it felt good to let him know how she felt. He held her hand as they talked for the next hour about the present and future.

They both turned towards the door as it opened.

"I knew that you would say yes, and there is no time like the present. Look who we found walking down the hallway." Violet, Harrison, and Frankie walked into the room, along with Minister Thornton, and a host of nurses and doctors, and Mikel's brother, Lance, and his family.

Violet walked over to the bed and kissed Avery's cheek. "Let me brush your hair back, baby, and let's put you on some lipstick."

"Let me guess, you all just happened to be walking down the hallway at this moment?" Avery giggled as her mother fussed over her.

"The Lord works in mysterious ways, my sister." Minister Thornton answered as he stood next to the bed.

Mikel hugged his family and turned to his father. "You did this, didn't you?"

Harrison shrugged. "Maybe, with a little help."

"I love you, Pops." Mikel hugged his father.

"I love you son, and I'm so proud of you."

"I'm proud of you too, little brother." Lance joined in on the hug.

Mikel walked back to Avery's bed. "Baby, do you want to do it now? We can wait until you are better and have a big wedding if that's what you want."

"Tomorrow isn't promised. I say let's do it." Avery smiled from ear to ear.

"Alright, ladies and gentlemen. Let's go ahead and get these two married so that Dr. Jones can receive the care she needs to walk out of this hospital. Praise God." Minister Thornton had the room filled with Amens and praise.

"A bride absolutely cannot get married without flowers." Tonya walked through the door with a beautiful bouquet of flowers, followed by Tony holding baby Alexandria, Brad and Katie, and Alicia and her man of the moment.

Avery's eyes filled with tears. "Thank you." She managed to whisper.

"Ok. Who gives this woman to be married to this man?" Minister Thornton asked.

"We do." The entire room said in unison before erupting in laughter.

Once everyone quieted down, Uncle Frankie spoke. "I do." He bent down to kiss Avery on the forehead and then shook Mikel's hand.

When it was time to exchange the rings, Avery remembered that she didn't have one for Mikel. "Oh, no, Mikel. I don't have a ring for you."

"Yes, you do." Harrison stepped forward and placed a gold wedding band in Avery's hand.

"Thanks, Pops." Mikel recognized the ring as his father's wedding band from his mother. He looked at his father's left hand and a new gold band adorned with diamonds rested on his ring finger. He looked at Violet's left hand and saw a huge diamond ring and wedding band on her ring finger.

Harrison pulled Violet in close to him. "Like you guys, we couldn't wait either." Harrison kissed Violet on the lips.

Avery smiled at her mother. She had never seen her as happy as she did right now.

"Under normal circumstances, this would be too weird, but I guess nothing about us is normal." Mikel laughed and so did everyone else.

"I now pronounce you husband and wife. Young man, you may kiss your bride." Mikel smiled before planting a passionate, yet gentle kiss on Avery's lips.

The room erupted in cheers and applause.

"I love you."

"Not as much as I love you, my wife."

EPILOGUE

|||||||||||||||||||||||||||||||||||||||||||||||||||||||||||||||||||||||||||||

Two Years Later

"Santos, Raven, come on. Let's go outside." Avery opened the door for the two dogs as they barreled out the front door to go outside to play. She laughed as she thought to herself that she was glad that she and Mikel added another dog to their family. The new Santos was almost as well trained as the original Santos, but he was still a puppy. A big, 120-pound puppy. Raven and Santos chased each other around the yard. Avery could hear Mikel edging up the yard as she walked to the mailbox. Smiling, she thought about how Mikel quitting the police force to go to medical school, and her cutting back hours at the hospital were both perfect choices for them. She opened the gate and went to the mailbox. She shuffled through the mail as she walked through the gate and back toward the house. Avery took notice of a plain white envelope. No return address, just addressed to her. No stamp, so someone obviously placed it in her mailbox. She opened the envelope and read the typed letter inside.

Your father's debt is now yours. You have ten days to get me two million dollars. I will leave another letter telling you where to make the drop.

X

Avery laughed as she neatly placed the letter back in the envelope. Santos stopped playing in the yard and ran over to Avery. He stood in front of her and growled towards the wooded area to the right of Avery. Looking in that direction, Avery placed her two fingers together mimicking a gun, and pulled the imaginary trigger towards the man who thought he was hiding out of sight on the edge of the property, outside of the gate. He dropped his binoculars and smiled.

"Crazy ass, chica. Just like your father."

As he turned to walk away, Santos started to charge. "Heel boy." Santos stopped dead in his tracks and came back to Avery. She stooped down and rubbed Santos' head. "We will let him live for now, boy. Come on." She trotted back towards the house, making her way towards Mikel. She made a mental note to activate the perimeter alarms again.

Avery waited for him to turn off the edger and then kissed him on the lips. "You ready for war?"

"Aww, hell. I guess so. We're in this shit together, right?" Mikel pulled her closer and kissed her passionately.

"Hell yeah, we are." She popped Mikel on the butt and surveyed the perimeter. Everything was fine. She nodded to Mikel, and he finished the yard work as she walked into the house and down to the basement. After placing a call on her cell phone, she waited for an answer on the other line.

"Mi corazon," Frankie answered.

"Hey, Uncle Frankie. Guess what?" Avery said.

"You're pregnant." Frankie offered.

"No sir. Not yet." Avery laughed. "Take another guess." Avery loaded the magazine in her gun.

Frankie didn't miss the distinct click of the magazine into the gun "Do you need me to protect you? Who is it?"

"Somebody named X. Do you know him?" Avery loaded a magazine into another gun. "Uncle Frankie?"

"We will be over in ten minutes. X is no joke, but if he wants a war with my baby girl, he will get it." Frankie started checking the magazines in his guns. He was thankful that he decided to move close to Avery and that Juan decided to join him. "And don't tell Adriana."

"Yes, sir. See you soon, Uncle Frankie." Ending the call Avery shot at the target, hearing her uncle in her ear like she always did. *Head shot... Go.* Emptying the gun, she smiled. "We will meet soon, Mr. X. I hope you have protection." Laughing she emptied another magazine into the target.

Printed in the United States
by Baker & Taylor Publisher Services